KILLER

ROBERT SILVERBERG

Black Gat Books • Eureka California

KILLER
Published by Black Gat Books
A division of Stark House Press
1315 H Street
Eureka, CA 95501, USA
griffinskye3@sbcglobal.net
www.starkhousepress.com

ISBN-13: 978-1-951473-68-6

Cover and text design by Jeff Vorzimmer, ¡caliente!design, Austin, Texas
Proofreading by Bill Kelly
Cover art by Ernest Chiriacka

PUBLISHER'S NOTE:
This is a work of fiction. Names, characters, places and incidents are either
the products of the author's imagination or used fictionally, and any
resemblance to actual persons, living or dead, events or locales, is entirely
coincidental.

First Stark House Press/Black Gat Edition: April 2022

"The best writer of fiction now breathing. When he wrote a mainstream novel, *Dying Inside*, it embodied and emboldened in its tragic force. And the erotic 'soft core' novels of his early career were flawless in their execution and force. The man set the bar for all of us in or out of the wilderness struggling to improve our work."

—Barry N. Malzberg

"Silverberg keeps things racing along at an entertaining pace."

—James Reasoner, *Rough Edges*

"Plenty of R-rated action to go around."

—Bruce Grossman, *Bookgasm*

"... compulsively readable."

–Michael Hemmingson

"Don Elliott is my kind of writer."

—Andrew Shaw, author of *Campus Tramp*

CHAPTER ONE

It was raining the day Lee Floyd pulled into New York City. He came in on the night bus from Cleveland, after traveling thirteen bumpy and sleepless hours across the Pennsylvania Turnpike. But when he stepped down from the bus, Floyd was wide-awake and razor-sharp, ready to do the job Howard Gorman was paying him to do.

First thing to do was see Gorman. Then get himself a girl to keep him company while he was in town. And then do the job.

Lee Floyd was ready.

The .38 was ready, too. It was sitting inside Floyd's brown alligator suitcase, wrapped up in a polo shirt. To look at him, you wouldn't think that Floyd was carrying a weapon in his suitcase, or that he had come to New York City to commit a murder. He looked like a college kid who was in New York for a fling. Floyd was small-boned, clean-faced, quiet, with flickering eyes that took in everything.

He looked around the bus terminal. Bright fluorescent lights, people hurrying back and forth. There was a coppery taste of lust in his mouth. New York was full of sexy girls, Floyd knew. He wanted one, and he wanted one fast. A tall one, with long legs and the kind of breasts that you had to spread your fingers out to hold all of, he thought. He could practically sense his need.

But first he had to call Gorman.

He stopped off in a telephone booth just across the way from the information counter, and dialed the number. The telephone rang five, six, seven times. Floyd held on, waiting, a muscle flickering tensely in his cheek. Finally Gorman answered.

"Hello? Howard Gorman speaking. Who is this,

please?" He sounded nervous.

"This is Lee Floyd here, Gorman. My bus just pulled in two minutes ago."

"Oh. Floyd." There was silence at the other end. The silence seemed to drag on for almost a minute.

"You don't sound glad to hear from me, Gorman," Floyd said crisply.

"I was just thinking."

Floyd said, irritated, "You aren't backing out of our arrangement, are you?"

"Of course not."

"Good. I wouldn't want to have come all the way in to New York just for the trip."

"Don't worry," Gorman said. "Everything's still as we arranged it."

"Good. Suppose you meet me for lunch in an hour or so, okay? We can talk over our arrangement then."

There was a harrumphing sound at the other end. "I already have an appointment for lunch," Gorman began. "A very important client who ..."

"Break it." Floyd said.

"But ..."

"I want to see you in an hour." The killer's flat, hard tones were designed to leave very little doubt that the statement was an order. Floyd waited a few seconds, then added, "Can it be managed?"

"I ... think so."

"Good," Floyd said. "I'm staying at the Hotel Ascot. You know where that is?"

"Yes."

"Suppose you meet me in the Ascot coffee shop at noon, then."

"I'll be there," said Gorman.

Floyd hung up. Gorman sounded scared and uneasy, but that was only to be expected, Floyd figured. A man took a big decision when he hired somebody to kill his wife, after all. It was just business for Lee Floyd, though.

Over to the hotel, now. Check in, get freshened up a little. See Gorman.

Then find a broad.

"Taxi!" Floyd yelled.

A cab pulled up. Floyd hustled through the rain to the hack. The rain was coming down harder than ever now, big gray pellets scudding diagonally out of the sky. The air was warm, muggily humid. Lousy weather, he thought. But it didn't rain forever.

He tossed his suitcase into the cab and climbed in.

"Hotel Ascot," he said.

"Lousy weather," said the cabbie.

"I was just thinking the same thing."

"You in town for a visit?"

"More or less," Floyd said.

"Alone?"

"That's right."

The cabbie was silent a moment. He steered his way through a jam of cars on Eighth Avenue, honking his horn furiously. Then he said, "You looking for some action, maybe?"

"Not if I have to pay for it," Floyd said.

"Oh. One of those guys."

"Why not? Anybody's got to pay for it this day and age, he's got something wrong with him."

"Yeah," the cabbie said, sighing. "But a guy's got to make a living, all the same. You'd be surprised, the kind of business I do peddling the girlies. If I wasn't disgusted by the idea, I'd quit the cab business and just be a pimp."

Floyd laughed. "I guess there are a lot of guys who have to pay for it."

"They figure it's easier on them than making a

pickup," the cabbie said. "Saves a lot of wear and tear on their nervous system. Never any doubts."

"If a guy knows what he's doing," Floyd said, "he doesn't need to have doubts."

"Hey, you're pretty sure of yourself, aren't you?"

"I've got reason to be," Floyd said. "I never have much trouble finding girls."

"Or making them?"

"Or making them," Floyd said.

The cab halted for a red light. The cabbie pulled a little booklet out of his jacket pocket and handed it back to Floyd. "Here," he said. "Take a look, anyway. Maybe you'll see something that interests you. These are the girls I got the representation for."

What he had handed Floyd was a little packet of glossy black-and-white photos, stapled together at the upper left hand corner. They showed girls. Nude girls, one to a photo. They were in a variety of provocative poses, the kind of saucy stuff you see in the girlie magazines, and a few shots that no magazine was likely to print. Most of the girls were built well, with big breasts and flat waists, but their faces were stupid, with dull eyes and silly grins. What could you expect, Floyd wondered?

He leafed through the packet. Nine girls altogether. He felt a little tickling sensation of lust at the sight of the unretouched photos. Stupid broads, all of them. But available. All he had to do was say the word and any one of the girls in these photos would be his.

For a price.

He handed the packet back at the next red light. "You got some pretty handsome hunks of flesh here," Floyd said.

"Ain't they, though?"

"What do you do, work on a percentage?"

"Yeah," the cabbie said. "Part of it in cash and part of it in merchandise."

"Lucky guy."

"You got to have business sense," the cabbie said. "That's all it takes. You sure I can't interest you in any of them, anyhow?"

"Not unless you're giving them away," Floyd said. "I never buy."

"Well, I guess I can't blame you," the cabbie said. "In a town like this, there are too many amateurs. But some guys prefer the pros."

"Not me," Floyd said.

He sat back and watched the rain. Great little town, New York. You'd expect the cabbies to be peddling flesh to strangers no matter what town you came to, but only in New York did they hand you a catalog of the goods. But Floyd wasn't buying. He was pretty confident that he could do okay on his own, for free.

Across town, in an apartment in a luxury building on Third Avenue, a girl named Marie was waking up.

She yawned. She stretched.

She flung the covers off and got to her feet.

She was nude, because that was the way Marie liked to sleep. Marie didn't like to wear clothes any more than she absolutely had to. She was a long-legged redhead, sleek and lush, with two round firm high breasts and a flaring waist and soft, dimpled, tender buttocks. She was twenty-three years old, and she would never look more beautiful in her life than she did right now.

She padded across the carpeted floor and into the bathroom. A frowsy, rumpled Marie looked back at her out of the mirror. Marie made a face at herself. Then she splashed cold water at her face—the one attached to her head, not the one in the mirror.

There, she thought. That's better.

Lots better.

With her eyes open now, she sized herself up in the mirror. Big firm breasts. Broad shoulders. Delicate collarbones. Lustrous hair. She grinned at herself. She winked at herself. She put her hands over her resilient breasts and gave them a good squeeze.

Then she stepped into the shower, and let the fine cascade of water descend. She held her body under it, enjoying the needle spray against her nipples, against the flat drum of her waist, against her legs.

It was a fine old life, Marie thought.

Lots of good loving, lots of good food, lots of good liquor. No worries. A rich old daddy like Howard Gorman to pay the bills. It was a nuisance having to go to bed with the fat old fool, but it was worth the discomfort. He paid her rent and covered her living expenses. What she pried out of Howard Gorman every month was a lot more than she could be making as a free-lance call girl, so why kick?

Besides, Gorman didn't monopolize her. There were plenty of hours of the day when she could get some fun in other quarters of the universe.

She got out of the shower and toweled herself dry. Her big breasts leaped and jiggled around as she gave herself a brisk rub-a-dub, down her back as far as her buttocks, then her legs. Naked, Marie strode back into the living room and looked out the window.

Raining. A dull, gray, miserable day.

Well, she wasn't going anywhere. She picked up the telephone, a little ivory-colored Princess phone, and dialed a number. It rang a few times at the other end. While she waited for her friend to answer, Marie idly cupped one of her ripe, heavy breasts, digging her fingertips casually into the yielding flesh. Then she let the hand wander down across her body, to her legs, and it rested there.

There was the sound of someone picking up the phone at the other end.

"Hello?"

"Dolores?"

"Marie?"

"You guessed it, baby. I wake you up?"

"Not really. It's a lousy day."

"That's outdoors," Marie said. "I'm indoors. You in a mood for fun?"

"You know I am. Always."

"So am I."

"Your place or mine?"

"Mine," Marie said. "It was your place the last time, remember?"

"That's right," said Dolores. "Okay. I'll come over. Have you had breakfast yet?"

"No. I just got up."

"Same here," Dolores said, "Wait till I get there, will you? We'll have breakfast together, okay?"

"Sure, honeybear. Sure."

"See you in ten minutes."

"Right."

Marie smiled. She put down the telephone. There was a sudden throbbing in her breasts and a pounding of desire in her arms. It was going to be a fun morning, she thought pleasantly. Good old Dolores. You could always count on Dolores for a quick romp in the hay on a rainy day.

It was a good life, Marie thought.

It was absolutely the greatest.

She gave her bare breasts another little squeeze, just for luck. Soon she'd have Dolores' boobs to squeeze instead, which would be more fun.

She walked into the kitchen. Time to see what was

in the fridge, she figured. Breakfast-time. Marie found an apron and tied it around her hips. It was a skimpy little thing that just covered her thighs. She looked down at herself, and saw her big breasts and flat waist, and then the little red apron, and when she looked over her shoulder she could see the pink cheeks of her buttocks sticking out where the apron didn't close in the rear. Marie giggled. The apron was cute. It was a gift from Howard. Dolores would appreciate it, Marie thought. She opened the refrigerator and began to rummage around.

Howard Gorman said, "I'm going out for a luncheon appointment. I'll be back about two o'clock."

His secretary nodded. "Yes, Mr. Gorman."

He cleared his desk, locked the drawer, and stood up. A glance out the window told him that it hadn't stopped raining. The leaden skies didn't help his mood any. He had been edgy and nervous and fretful all day, and the telephone call from the killer had only made things worse.

But the tension would be over soon, Gorman thought. The long nightmare would end.

The tough guy from the west would kill Ethel. For a price, probably a stiff price, but Gorman didn't worry about that. He had plenty of money. Now he wanted to trade some of that money for freedom.

Freedom to marry Marie.

To have her every night, not just when he could manage to get away. To possess her. To fill his hands with the wondrous flesh of her breasts. Her lips against his, her tongue touching his. Her long, lean body aching in passion.

Marie. His.

As soon as Ethel was out of the way.

Would there be any risk? Gorman didn't think so. This man was supposed to be a pro. Gorman appreciated professionalism. A pro, in any field, was a man who did exactly what he was paid to do, and did it to the complete satisfaction of his employer.

Ethel would die, then. And Gorman would have Marie all the time.

Some of Gorman's tension ebbed away at that thought. Some, but not all. The fact still remained that he was getting himself involved in murder, and that was a brand new field for Howard Gorman. Nobody got rich without breaking some laws, and Gorman had broken plenty in his day, but they hadn't been criminal laws. You connived, you manipulated, you lied, you swindled here and there, and you got rich. But you didn't murder. This would be murder.

But it was the only way. Ethel seemed strong enough to live forever. And Gorman couldn't wait forever. Not with Marie to be had. Marie of the rich auburn hair, Marie of the breasts like swollen melons, the long shapely legs, the firm, milk-white buttocks.

Gorman pulled his raincoat tight around him and flagged down a taxi.

"Hotel Ascot," he said.

Lee Floyd checked in at the desk. He had already made reservations, writing from Cleveland ahead of time. He had picked the hotel carefully. There was a buyers' convention in progress there; it would serve adequately as camouflage, swallowing up all out-of-towners.

"Front!" the desk clerk called.

Floyd and the bellhop went upstairs. He had a room on the eleventh floor. It was neat, not too freshly painted, but that was all right. Floyd wasn't buying it, he was just moving in for a few days.

"Here are the controls for the air conditioner," the bellhop said. "You want it colder in here, you just turn this dial to the right."

Floyd nodded. He gave the boy a quarter, got the keys, and turned the dial to the right. That would suck some of the humidity out of the room.

He opened his suitcase. The gun was the first thing he went for. It was snug and safe. He unpacked everything carefully. The rain still clattered down outside. There was a drumbeat of lust-tension in the little killer's body. Those naked pictures the cabbie had shown him had stirred him up more than he cared to admit.

Another few hours, he thought, He'd pick someone up and get some action fast.

Even if he had to pay. The important thing was getting some when he wanted and he needed that now. Sex was a good steadier of the nerves.

He figured on spending five or six days in New York on this stint. That was more than he needed, strictly speaking, to pull off a killing. But he liked to go about it in a business-like way. There would be a time-spread of a few days on either side of the job itself, to throw any pursuers off the trail. Floyd knew his stuff. That was why Howard Gorman had reached all the way to Cleveland to hire him, when he had decided that the time at last had come to get rid of his wife.

Floyd shaved and changed his shirt. He liked to be neat and presentable at all times. The usual hoodlum stereotype of behavior didn't appeal to him at all. He was a businessman, not a slob or a punk.

At ten minutes to twelve he went downstairs and found the hotel's coffee lounge. It was pretty crowded, the noonday business trade. A captain looked at him.

"I'd like to reserve a table for two," Floyd said.

"Certainly, sir."

"Let's say for five after twelve. I'm waiting for someone to show up."

Floyd parked himself by the entrance to the coffee lounge. Seven minutes later a fat and florid man in his mid-fifties came along. He was puffing and red-faced, and he looked nervous and hunted and very ill at ease. Floyd grinned. The client had arrived.

He stepped out from the side of a potted rubber plant and said, smiling, "Mr. Gorman?"

The fat man jumped in surprise, as though Floyd had kicked him smartly.

Then he recovered and managed to flash a clumsy smile. "Why yes. Are you Mr. Floyd?"

"That's right. Let's go in, shall we?"

He led the way to the table he had reserved. It was in the back, near the window facing out on the street. Just about all the other tables were filled now. Floyd always believed in arranging for things in advance— whether it was a hotel room, a restaurant table, or an alibi for a murder assignment.

They sat down.

Floyd said, "Let's not talk business right away. Let's have lunch first."

"Anything you say," Gorman muttered.

The waiter came over. Floyd studied the menu with care. He was hungry.

Food first. Then business.

Then some love.

CHAPTER TWO

It was a fairly extensive menu, and Floyd didn't stint himself when ordering. His lean, wiry body packed a lot of energy, and he needed solid meals. He treated himself to a sirloin and cold mashed potatoes with sour cream and a couple of bottles of imported beer. Gorman ordered a salad plate and looked longingly at Floyd's cold mashed potatoes.

Gorman looked sick, Floyd thought. His fleshy face was beaded with shining dabs of sweat; his bald, shiny head was even shinier with moisture. Although he had ordered a light meal, he only toyed with it, nibbling at a piece of tomato and a slice of hard-boiled egg. Floyd, meanwhile, did justice to his full course luncheon. The trip in from Cleveland had given him a keen appetite.

The businessman kept eyeing Floyd unhappily through the meal, as they talked. They talked all around the world, talked about the weather and the stock market and the baseball standings. It was an arm's-length conversation, the uncomfortable talk of two men who didn't know each other very well and who had almost nothing in common.

Floyd could practically read Gorman's mind. The fat man was obviously thinking, *This is a killer. I'm eating lunch with a common gunman. With the man who is going to murder my wife for me.*

The disdain came across, clear and strong.

Floyd didn't mind. He knew that a professional killer didn't have much social status. Even a fat, greedy businessman like Gorman could look down his nose at him, because he was a man of the underworld.

They finished eating.

"You want some more beer?" Gorman asked.

"No," Floyd said. "I've had enough. I think we ought to be moving along."

"Whenever you say."

"Now."

Not a word had been said yet about the arrangement between them, about the little job of murder that had to be done. Floyd wasn't in a rush about that.

The check arrived. Floyd glanced at it but left it lying on the table, and Gorman paid it without a word. Floyd noticed the size of the bankroll that Gorman pulled out. He saw the businessman leave a hefty tip, too, rounding it off to the nearest dollar without worrying about the exact percentage. That was a healthy sign, Floyd thought. It meant that Gorman wasn't trying to conceal the fact that he had money. They still hadn't negotiated the price for this deal.

As they passed out of the coffee-shop Floyd said in bland tones, "I think you've got a very strong selling-point there, Howard. Would you like to come up to my room now and we can clinch the deal there?"

"What? Oh." Gorman looked very pale. He glanced at his watch. "I really don't have time—"

He's afraid to get into a room alone with me, Floyd thought. He grinned at Gorman disarmingly. "Oh, come now, Howard," he said. "How many times in your life do you make a deal of this sort?" Something cold came into his face, a look intended for Gorman alone. The pretense that this was a businessman's lunch was for any busy ears that happened to be in the neighborhood.

"Very well," Gorman said heavily.

They walked across the lobby toward the elevator. Floyd flashed a quick smile as they got in.

"We can get the terms settled upstairs," he said.

The doorbell rang. Still nude except for the little apron and a pair of high-heeled shoes that she had donned as a gag, Marie went to the door. She looked like a fashionable maid who had forgotten to put on most of her uniform.

She opened the door. Dolores grinned at her.

"Hi," she said. "I like the costume!"

"It's my new summer special," Marie said. "Come on in. You must be all wet."

"It's raining horses and elephants out there," Dolores said. She shook herself, and droplets of water flew from her, some of them landing on Marie's bare skin. Marie giggled as a cold raindrop hit her in the nipple. She took Dolores' raincoat from her, and Dolores went inside.

The two girls were similar in many ways. They were both in their early twenties. They were both stunningly good looking. They were both breasty and leggy. Marie was a redhead, Dolores a brunette, but they resembled each other physically and facially enough to seem like sisters.

They had other things in common, too. Both girls supported themselves by what men gave them.

And both girls enjoyed a little offbeat love of the Lesbian variety.

They went into the kitchen. "I was just pouring some orange juice," Marie said. "And the coffee's just about ready, I guess."

"I love that apron," Dolores said.

"Isn't it cute?"

"And I love what's sticking out behind it, too." She laughed and reached out, putting her hands on the bare pink cool rounds of Marie's exposed buttocks and letting her fingers slide quickly over the satiny skin.

Marie grinned. She glanced at Dolores, who was wearing a tight cashmere sweater and a pair of plaid slacks that clung to the contours of her hips and buttocks like a skin graft. She winked. Dolores winked back.

Marie cracked a couple of eggs. "Is scrambled okay?" she asked.

"Any way," Dolores said. She came up behind Marie and nuzzled her lips against the nape of Marie's neck. She slid her hands around front, cupping them over the ripe, high, lush thrusts of Marie's nude breasts. Marie's nipples began to ache. She was already excited. The mere fact of being almost naked in front of Dolores was enough to cause that. But the touch of Dolores' hands sent thrills of anticipated ecstasy through her.

Marie said, "Were you with Paul last night?"

"Yeah." Delores said. "What a kook."

"He's a rich kook, isn't he?"

"Even so ...!"

"What did he pull last night?"

Dolores laughed wearily. "Oh, it was a good one last night. He brought along some crazy kind of rubber underwear for me. It was like a suit of armor that covered me from knee to shoulders, except that there were holes in it for my breasts to stick out, and it was open in back."

"They sell those nutty things downtown," Marie said. "I once knew a guy who went in for that stuff."

"He laced me into it, and it hurt like blazes, believe me. I had red marks in my skin for hours afterward. Then he made me march up and down in the thing, and jump so my breasts jiggled around, and bend over so he could spank me."

"The cockeyed ways men get their kicks."

"He's a lulu," Dolores said.

"But a rich lulu."

"Yeah. He gave me five hundred bucks last night and I think he's getting me an emerald ring."

"You'd wear a lot of rubber underwear for that, I bet," Marie said.

"Darned right I would." She shrugged. "What's new with Howard?"

"I'm seeing him tonight."

"Anything doing on the marriage front?"

"I don't know," Marie said. "We're hoping that his wife's health will take a sudden turn for the worse."

"That would be a real good break for you," Dolores said. "Marrying a fat old coot like that. Wear him out in bed, give him a heart attack in two or three years—you'd be sitting pretty, wouldn't you?"

"Don't think I haven't thought about it," Marie said. She took the pan of eggs from the stove. Her breasts swayed as she bent forward to put them in the plates. She smiled at Dolores. "Let's eat."

"I'm famished."

"So am I."

"Wait a second," Dolores said. "Let me get my clothes off. I might as well make myself comfortable."

"You might as well," Marie said. "And it'll save time later on, too."

Floyd very carefully locked the door of his hotel room. It was an act that didn't decrease Gorman's uneasiness at all. He turned around to face the other man.

He said, "I think we can talk plainly in here. You really want to get rid of your wife, huh?"

"I do," Gorman said.

Guilt-shadows crossed the fat man's face. He

knotted his pink, pudgy, well-manicured hands together and leaned forward in his armchair.

"You want to get rid of her bad enough to pay five thousand dollars for the job?" Floyd asked.

Gorman looked puzzled. "Marie told me it would be only three thousand."

Floyd sighed in quiet amusement. "Whoever Marie is, you can tell her that her information's cockeyed. My rate for that kind of job is five thousand, and it always has been. I'm not boosting it special for you. And who's this Marie, anyway?"

Reddening, Gorman said, "She's the girl I—I want to marry. As soon as Ethel's gone. She used to dance at a big night club here. I'm keeping her these days."

The pieces began to fall into place for Lee Floyd. He always liked to have a full grasp of the situation before he began a job, so that he knew who was what in relation to whom. It helped, when the time came to set up the job. So now he knew that Gorman's girl friend was named Marie. Marie was the contact who had put him in touch with Gorman to do the job.

Floyd took a bottle of bourbon from his suitcase and pointed it toward Gorman like a gun.

"Drink?" he asked.

"No, thanks," Gorman said.

Floyd put the bottle away, shrugging.

Gorman said quickly, "But I don't mind if you have one, though. Don't deprive yourself on my account."

The killer stared squarely at his client. "I never drink anything stronger than beer," he said. "It's bad for the reflexes. And I live by my reflexes, Gorman. I keep this bottle here to offer to others."

"You're quite the businessman, aren't you?" said Gorman admiringly. "I imagine you'd probably be vice-president of some big corporation by now, if you had chosen some other line of work than—than—" He faltered.

"Than killing?" Floyd filled in. "Maybe so." He folded his arms tightly. "Did your Marie know me by name, Gorman?"

"No. She just said that there was someone in Cleveland who could—ah—end our trouble for us. She knew someone who could get in touch with you, or rather someone who could get in touch with someone who—well, you understand. Through channels. Marie told me that she thought you charged three thousand."

"I charge five," Floyd said. "If you think that's too much for you, say so right now before we waste any more of our time."

Gorman was silent for a moment. Then he said in a kind of drawl, "I can afford five thousand dollars for the job, I guess."

"You could afford fifty thousand for what you want done," Floyd told him bluntly. "You're lucky I'm only charging five. But I don't believe in extortion. That's one crime I have no sympathy with. My fee is my fee, and I stick to it, and I don't raise it or lower it depending on what I think the traffic will bear, like some guys I know."

"How do you want the money paid? I could write a check for some of it now, if —"

"No. Cash, please," Floyd said icily. "Large checks present certain problems of cashing, and require unpleasant detail like signatures."

"Of course. I didn't think—"

"Today is Thursday. Send $2,500 in cash by special messenger to my hotel tomorrow morning. Have the money here by ten o'clock. Can you manage that?"

Gorman nodded.

"As for the other half of the fee," Floyd said, "that's to come similarly on Saturday morning, no later than ten o'clock."

"When will the job be done?"

"By midnight on Saturday."

"And how long will you stay in New York after that?" Gorman asked.

"Anything I do after midnight Saturday," Floyd said with cold precision, "is no longer any concern of yours. Clear? You will please forget that I ever existed. Remember that my life and yours will be forever bound after this little ... business deal. You're just as subject to the chair as I am for your wife's murder. So keep your wits about you after Saturday night."

"I'm planning to go away," Gorman said. "I'll leave as soon as I can, after the—ahem—the tragedy. I'll go to Bermuda. Marie will go down there separately. We'll meet there, strictly by accident, two strangers at the same hotel. After a few months, we can return and get married. If it looks strange to anyone, I'll explain that I just couldn't live alone after Ethel's death."

"That sounds reasonable enough," Floyd said. "You have a passport?"

"Of course. So does Marie. I took mine out last year for a business trip. Marie just got hers a month or so ago, when we began talking about this."

"And the transportation?"

"I have passage booked on a luxury cruiser. Marie will fly down to Bermuda tourist class a week ahead of me. No one will suspect any possible connection between us, I'm pretty sure."

Floyd smiled. "I could get to like you, Gorman. You know how to plan things. I admire a shrewd planner. You'd do well in my business."

"I suppose that's a compliment," Gorman said. "Well, thanks." He looked much less nervous now that everything was settled. He rose, stretching, and complacently patted his paunch. "Time to get back to the office, now. I guess that the arrangements are complete. You have the address, don't you?"

Floyd nodded.

"All right," Gorman said. "I'll have half the cash for you tomorrow morning."

Marie watched with interest as Dolores eased herself out of her clothes. Off came the cashmere sweater. Dolores winked and unhooked her brassiere, the cups dropping away from the high, flawless rounds of her bosom. Two white peaks of flesh, tipped with flame-red nipples that were standing taut, came into view.

Dolores unzipped the plaid slacks and pulled them down over her ample hips. Only filmy green panties hid her nudity now, but not for long. She rolled them down, inch by inch, laying bare the gently rounded curve of her waist with its deep-socketed navel, and the fullness of her hips and the lush inviting legs. She turned to toss the panties aside, giving Marie a view of her firm-fleshed buttocks.

Desire began to churn for Marie. She could appreciate a beautiful girl as much as any guy could. And Dolores was beautiful, with her pale skin and her dark hair and her voluptuous figure.

"Now I'm nuder than you are," Dolores said. "At least you've got an apron on."

"I'm shy."

"Yeah. That must be the reason."

"Have some scrambled eggs."

"Glad to," Dolores said.

They ate heartily. Both girls had healthy appetites.

They got plenty of sleep, plenty of exercise, and they liked to eat. The coffee pot went around a couple of times. Then they cleared the dishes away.

It was around noon, now, on a rainy Thursday. The rest of New York City was busy working. Not Marie. Not Dolores. They had their daddies to ante up the bills. That left them with lots of free time on their hands. And other things on their hands too, like each other's bosoms.

"Let's go get cozy," Dolores suggested, her voice a provocative purr.

"Yeah!" Marie agreed.

Breasts bobbling, buttocks switching from side to side, the two tall nude girls scurried into the bedroom. Marie was tense with expectancy.

"Lie down," Dolores said. "Let me give you one of my special massages."

"Just what I'm in the mood for."

"Here we go."

Marie sprawled out face down on the bed, her heavy breasts flattening into the bedding. Dolores rose to her knees and settled down. Marie could feel the warmth of Dolores. A moment later, Dolores' fingers began to move in the muscles of Marie's back and neck and shoulders.

"That feels great," Marie sighed.

"Feels pretty good from this end too."

This is terrific, Marie thought. Dolores had real skill as a masseuse. It was the old dodge, calling a prostitute a masseuse, but in this case Dolores knew her stuff. The probing fingers found the tension-spots, kneaded them, worked them out with professional expertise. It was wonderfully relaxing, so marvelously soothing.

Marie drifted into a dreamy haze of relaxation. Dolores worked back and forth, back and forth, every touch of her adept hands bringing new ease and calmness.

And then the rotating hands began to move to new places. Down, past Marie's armpits, to the sides of her breasts. They worked their way underneath Marie's body, and suddenly her breasts were in Dolores' hands, and Dolores was cupping the firm young swells of flesh, trapping the nipples, caressing from side to side.

Marie smiled. She purred in contentment. The feel of Dolores' hands was a wonderful sensation.

Marie felt Dolores' warm breath against the nape of her neck. Dolores whispered, "You're so beautiful ... I love your breasts, Marie. I wish I could hold them forever."

"They're all yours, baby."

"I love them," Dolores whispered.

She brought her lips to the lobe of Marie's ear, and nibbled playfully. Marie began to gasp. As she lay face down with Dolores pressing her, and as the lithe kiss continued to touch her ear, Marie's passionate yearnings started to course over her. Her nipples at Dolores' eager grasp, were rigid with desire.

Dolores began to move the length of Marie— kissing as she went. She drew a warm line of kisses between Marie's shoulder blades, then lingered for a moment in the small of her back. Then she continued. Marie trembled with passion. Dolores continued still further, pressing now behind Marie's knees.

Dolores' lips flashed once like a serpent.

Marie gasped.

Men had tried this of course, but they never seemed to have the skill of another woman. Dolores was an expert at lovemaking. She seemed to know exactly how to give the greatest pleasure.

The caress lasted an eternity.

Swiftly, Marie felt weak and trembling and dizzy. She lay limply as the currents of desire pounded over her frame.

"Turn over now," Dolores whispered.

Marie smiled and complied. Again Dolores moved toward Marie, again the agile lips worked devilishly. Marie responded with quiverings. Chills ran the length of her body. Now she began to move herself.

Marie's hands reached out. They found the massive globes of Dolores' breasts, cupped them, held onto them. They were firm but yielding, almost like foam rubber. The nipples were large and swollen, like Marie's own. Marie held the dark-haired girl's breasts to a tight grip. Dolores hissed in pleasure and moved until they were practically face to face.

"Love me now," Dolores murmured.

Marie lowered her head. She began to kiss. Dolores gasped in pleasure for a while. Then she turned so that they could give pleasure to one another at the same time. The long kiss continued until both were dizzy with desire.

Then, suddenly, there was a flurry of rearranging. Their lips met.

The bed protested groaningly, but neither paid the slightest bit of attention. With frenzied haste, they scaled the ladder of passion. Marie sensed the familiar gathering storm of delight—and gave herself up completely as the storm of passion struck. It swirled around her, raging tempestuously, and she let herself drown—let the tide burst over her. She heard Dolores gasp and cry out in ecstasy at the sublime moment. Perspiration drenched their satiny skins, and they lay quietly on the swells of their passion, all fury spent, all frenzy burned away in the afterglow.

Marie lightly kissed Dolores' breasts, first one,

then the other.

"That was fun," she whispered.

CHAPTER THREE

After Gorman had gone, Floyd stood by the window a while, peering down into the streets of mid-Manhattan, which were swarming with people in spite of the rain.

Today was Thursday. On Saturday he would do the job Howard Gorman wanted him to do. And on Tuesday next he would leave New York, five thousand dollars richer minus the trifling cost of bus-fare and bullets.

It was a pretty good way to earn a living, he thought.

It was a lot better than the squalid two-bit thievery in a Chicago slum where you had to jump, and jump fast, if you wanted to eat that night.

Floyd had been a good thief in his youth. In his thieving days he had never gone hungry and he had never served time. But he had never gotten very far ahead of the raw expenses of living, either.

Then somebody told him that he had killer nerves. "You ought to be hiring yourself out," he was told. "Pick up contracts all over the country."

It was good advice. Lee Floyd took it and went into the murder business. And he was a success at it. He was the deadliest killing machine in the Middle West and maybe in the country. He performed his duties with a cold, emotionless aplomb. Only a few people knew where to reach him—but, somehow, whenever a job needed to be done, Lee Floyd was tapped for it.

He thought about this job.

Five thousand bucks, just for burning the flabby wife of a rich businessman, so that the rich man could enjoy a couple of years of renewed youth with some long-legged youngster with a good eye for the old bank account.

Well, Floyd thought, the deal probably made sense to Gorman. And as long as the cash was on the line, the job would be done quickly and smoothly. He had the strategy all figured out. It was going to be one of his standard routines: burglar breaks into the home of wealthy suburbanite; Mrs. Howard Gorman shot and killed while attempting to defend her jewels. Quick, neat ... and while the police puzzled around for a while looking for the burglar-killer, Floyd would be on his way west with his five grand fee and Gorman would be happily winging toward a second honeymoon in the islands.

An easy kind of business, he thought.

Thursday, Friday, Saturday, Sunday, Monday, Tuesday. Six days, a harmless old female shot to death, and five grand earned. Floyd shrugged. He looked out the window. It was still raining, but starting to taper off.

Time to get himself a girl for the evening, now. As soon as the rain stopped.

Time to go quail-hunting.

He fixed his tie, and combed his hair. He grinned into the bathroom mirror. The image grinned back at him in an unfriendly way.

He went out.

The air had a muggy, humid, clammy touch to it, a hangover from all the rain. But the sun was shining. Floyd walked slowly, heading no place in particular. It was three in the afternoon, and there were plenty of people around, rushing to and fro. He ambled across Park Avenue and strolled west on 54th Street.

Then he caught sight of a girl.

Something about her told Floyd that she could be had. It was a kind of sixth sense that the killer had when it came to girls. This one looked single, somehow. She had a ring on her finger, but it wasn't an engagement ring or a wedding ring, just a ring. She was dressed in a casual, unmarried-looking way, too. A pleated skirt, a corduroy jacket through which a blue blouse could be seen. Young: twenty-five at the most, he figured. Straw-colored hair, cut fairly short and bobbed into bangs in front. Blue eyes that somehow didn't look innocent, but simply playful.

She was carrying one of those huge flat leather cases that freelance artists carry their work around in. Instantly Floyd had her pegged. She was an illustrator, he figured. Making the rounds with her art samples. Maybe she was finished for the day, going home.

He followed her.

He hadn't trailed her for more than ten paces when she made a sudden left turn and disappeared into a bar. No, Floyd corrected himself, not a bar. Here, half a block east of Madison Avenue, they called them cocktail lounges. He went right on in after her.

It was a dark, atmospheric place decked out to look like an English pub. A sophisticated bar for sophisticated New Yorkers, Floyd figured. It was so dimly lit that for a moment he had trouble catching sight of the girl, and then he saw her, sitting at the bar with her big leather satchel parked against one of her knees.

Floyd wasn't bashful. He knew that he had a knack for women, that there was something about his lean face with its sharp cheekbones and deep, soulful eyes that made them want to hop into bed with him the moment he looked at them. So he wasn't afraid of getting slapped. He walked over to the bar stool next to the girl and sat down on it.

"Hi," he said. "Nice of the rain to let up finally,

wasn't it?"

She turned and looked at him. There was a chill in the glance, the automatic chill of the unescorted New York girl getting set to block a pass, but then Floyd's appeal seemed to register on her, and she defrosted visibly. The whole transition had taken perhaps a fifth of a second.

"I thought it would never stop," she said. "And I had all kinds of places to see."

"It always stops sooner or later," Floyd said. "That's the good thing about rain. Can I buy you a drink?"

"That's usually the prologue to an immoral proposal in this city."

"I wouldn't know, I'm not from this city."

"You don't sound like you are. Where are you from?" she asked.

"One question at a time. Can I buy you a drink?"

"Is that an immoral proposal or isn't it?"

"It's a moral proposal," he said. "Which may be followed by immoral proposals later on. Yes or no?"

"Yes."

"What?"

"Stout," she said.

"What about your girlish figure?"

"A few calories won't hurt me," she said.

He signalled to the bartender. "One stout for the lady, and one Heinekens for me."

She said, "That leaves one question hanging in the air. Where are you from?"

"Columbus, Ohio," he said, figuring that was as good as anywhere to be from. "Now you owe me a question. What's your name?"

"Alice Henries. You?"

"Tom Wayte," he said, using one of his handy jiffy aliases.

"Hello, Tom."

"Hello, Alice."

The drinks arrived. They grinned at each other. Floyd knew that he was going to score, and it was a comforting thing to know.

She said, "What do you do?"

"I'm an engineer."

"Electronics?"

"Civil," he said. "I design sewers."

"How fascinating!"

"Do you really think so?"

"No," she said. "I don't. I just said it to be polite, as a matter of fact."

"It really is fascinating," Floyd said. "I could sit here for hours telling you how interesting it is to design sewers, believe it or not."

"I'll take your word for it."

"And you're an artist?" he said.

"How'd you know?"

"By the big leather whatzis parked down next to your leg," he said. "What's it full of? Sketches?"

"Illustrations. Magazine illustrations."

"I'd like to see some of your illustrations."

She grinned. "That's a switch. You're inviting yourself up to see some of my etchings."

"But I did it in a moral way."

"Very moral," Alice said. "I could use another stout, by the way."

"Terribly fattening stuff."

"I know. That's why they call it what they do. I could use another one anyway."

"How do you stay so slim if you drink so much stout?" Floyd asked.

"I get lots of exercise," she said. "When I'm not illustrating science fiction magazines, I have a part-time job as a nightclub bouncer. You ought to see me in action some time."

"I hope to," Floyd said. "What are you doing for dinner tonight?"

"Having it with you."

"It's all arranged, is it?"

"Sure."

It was. They had a few more beers at the pub, and then she took him over to her apartment. But not to make love. That would come afterward, she made that quite clear. She had a nice little bachelor-girl place just east of Lexington, three small rooms. When she took off her corduroy jacket, Floyd saw that she was built the way he liked. Firm ripe breasts pushed her blouse outward.

"I'm going to wash up," she said. "You can look through my drawings, if you want."

He settled down on the living room couch. She went into the bathroom. The illustrations looked pretty good to him, though he couldn't make much sense out of the eight-eyed monsters and the soaring rocket ships. At least she looked like a pro with India ink, and Floyd admired professionalism in whatever field it happened to be.

While he was waiting for her to come out, he was on the receiving end of a little unexpected treat. A gust of wind came sweeping out of New Jersey, through the open window of her apartment, and nudged the bathroom door open. Floyd happened to be looking that way, and he saw her.

She had taken her blouse and brassiere off, and was bent forward over the sink, washing herself. He saw in profile her tawny, round, rosy-tipped breasts.

She was cool about that. She straightened up and turned around, so that for a fraction of a second he had the front view of her bare breasts. Then she pushed the door closed, and that was that. Droplets of sweat had broken out on Floyd's forehead. He let out his breath.

She came out of the bathroom a few minutes later, carrying her blouse, her breasts covered by a towel. "I'll be just a minute more," she said. She didn't seem at all embarrassed by the little episode of the naked breasts.

She went into the bedroom and closed the door. Floyd watched it hopefully, but it didn't blow open. When she came out, she had left the pleated skirt behind, and she was wearing a one-piece dark green dress that stunningly set off the curves of her body. She looked a whole lot less kookie than she had in her jaunty street clothes.

"Let's go," she said. "I'm hungry."

"So am I. Where are we going?"

"There's a little Italian restaurant down the block where we can get a good meal," she said. "You like Italian food, don't you?"

"Sure. Fine idea."

"And then we can come back here afterward," she said in a tone that left no doubts about what would take place when they did.

"That's an even better idea," Floyd said.

Marie put a dab of perfume against the ripe hills of her breasts, and clipped her earrings on. Howard would be here any moment, the old goat. She wanted to look her best for him. For old Pappy Howard. He paid the bills, and he had a right to see her at her best, she figured.

Of course, it was a waste of time to dress up for Gorman, Marie thought. He lost so little time in getting her clothes off her once he arrived. But the least she could do was look pretty for him when he showed up. At the price he was paying for her company, she could make the effort.

The doorbell rang.

"Coming!" Marie sang out.

She let him in. He gave her a simpering smile and took her into his arms.

"Marie, darling," he murmured.

His fat lips crushed against hers. His soft, pudgy hands groped for her breasts, found them, squeezed them roughly.

Marie suppressed her shudders of revulsion. The old goat, she thought, as she wriggled voluptuously in a convincing counterfeit of passion.

They broke the clinch. He was flushed and panting.

"You're so beautiful, Marie. You look so lovely tonight," he said.

She smiled at him. They went into her living room. Not too many hours before, Marie and Dolores had been entangling their nude, breasty bodies in this apartment, but Howard Gorman didn't need to know that.

She fixed a drink for him, and one for herself. He sat down heavily on the couch and loosened his shoes. He didn't seem in any hurry to get down to business tonight, Marie thought. He looked a little tired.

He took a few sips of his drink. Then he said, "It's all arranged, Marie."

"What is?"

"Ethel. Her—demise."

"You made the deal, huh?"

Gorman nodded. "The man you recommended came in from Cleveland this morning. Lee Floyd. I met him for lunch at the Ascot. That's where he's staying. I told him what I wanted him to do, and he told me how much it would be, and we struck a deal.”

"When does it happen?”

"Saturday.”

"Will it be ready?”

"For him, maybe,” Gorman said. "Not for me. He's a real professional, Marie. He seems to be able to handle himself very well. So as of Saturday I'll be a free man.”

Marie beamed at him. Visions of dollar signs danced in her head.

"And then?”

"Then I go to Bermuda to recuperate from the shock of Ethel's death. And you happen to be there. And we happen to meet. And we fall in love, and get married, and live happily ever after. How does that sound?”

"It sounds glorious, Howard,” Marie breathed. "Come here, darling.”

She went to him and sat on his knees. She opened his shirt, pulled down his tie. He slipped his arm around her and caressed her breasts for a while. He began to breathe hard. He put one hand on her knee and slid it along. The hand working, exciting her.

Then he said, "Get into your costume now, Marie.”

She nodded and got to her feet. He beamed at her like a little boy about to get his Christmas present. Marie walked into the bedroom and closed the door.

She began to undress.

So she was going to get married, she thought. Become Mrs. Howard Gorman. Well, well. Wasn't that a pleasant way to get rich?

Gorman was fiftyish and fat. His health wasn't too good. He couldn't last long. He had no children and he had lots of money. All in all, the situation seemed like a highly attractive one.

Of course, there was the business of Gorman's style of lovemaking...

Well, she could tolerate that if she had to. He was a kook, but most middle-aged men that she had known developed some kind of quirk. What she hoped for was getting him so excited in bed that he'd have a coronary. And be rid of him quickly and quietly. She figured she could stir him into a death frenzy if she were his wife and shared his bed night after night.

But even so, the thought of having to make love to Howard Gorman made her sick to her stomach. She didn't do this for fun. This was strictly a cash proposition for Marie.

She peeled out of her garments. Took everything off, even her bra, panties, and stockings. Just as she thought: it had been a waste of time to dress up for him. Naked, her full breasts swaying, she went to the closet and took out the special costume that Gorman insisted she wear while she loved.

This afternoon Dolores had talked about the man who was keeping *her*, and the odd rig he made her don. Marie hadn't felt like mentioning it, but Gorman insisted on pretty much the same kind of outfit. Maybe they read the same textbooks of perversion, Marie figured.

She got into the weird outfit now. It consisted of a bra, a garter-belt, and stockings. But the bra had had its cups cut out, so that it consisted just of rims through which her breasts protruded, and the rims were far too small for the lush abundance of those two mounds of flesh. They cut cruelly into the soft flesh of her breasts. Gorman liked that. He enjoyed watching her suffer. The garter-belt too was a special affair, which laced instead of hooked. It sliced brutally into the flesh of her hips and upper buttocks.

The stockings were no sheer nylons, but some sort of rubber tubes.

And finally she took the leather whip from its hiding place in the closet.

They had been playing this game since Gorman first had made her his mistress. He had told her that the only way he could get real pleasure was by staging this little charade.

Marie had to pose as a slave girl. Gorman was her master. She had committed some misdeed, and he was going to take off all his clothing and whip her. When he had punished her sufficiently, he would feel sorry for her and then he would be able to make love to her.

It struck Marie as a silly and sinister game. But she had no way of getting out of playing it. Besides, she found it oddly stimulating to be whipped. That was the most peculiar part of all, that she seemed to enjoy having him whip her. Even the pain of wearing the tight garments added to the pleasure.

She went back into the living room. The points of her breasts stood out stiffly from the constricting bra. Gorman had taken off all his clothes and piled them neatly on a chair. Now he stood next to the couch, arms folded as he waited for her, a fat, sloppy-looking man with a soft body and strangely thin, blue-veined legs.

Marie fell into her role. She held the whip out toward him.

"Here is the whip, master. Punish me! Whip me hard! I've been a bad girl, master. Whip me!"

CHAPTER FOUR

The Italian restaurant where Lee Floyd and his blonde pickup had gone for dinner had turned out to be a good, inexpensive place where the food was hearty and abundant. He was in a good mood as they returned to Alice's place, about nine o'clock. He was well fed, he was about to go to bed with a handsome and intelligent girl, and he had an easy contract to fulfill here in New York.

Alice seemed to like him. Good for her, he thought. He had really snowed her with that civil engineer bit. She'd flip if she knew what he really did for a living, he thought. But of course she'd never know. They would never meet again. Floyd didn't believe in getting permanently involved with girls.

Evidently Alice didn't believe in long-term arrangements, either. He gathered from her conversation that she was an uninhibited, adventurous kind of girl who liked her freedom, and who didn't mind being picked up and taken to bed by interesting strangers.

Fine, Floyd thought.

Couldn't be better.

She unlocked her apartment and they went in. "I'm going to get into something comfortable," she said. "Wait—I'll put some music on. You can help yourself to the drinks if you want."

She switched on the FM. Soft string music filtered into the room. Floyd rummaged around in the liquor cabinet, but it was all hard stuff, which he didn't touch. He went into the kitchen. As he expected, there were bottles of stout in the refrigerator. He opened two of them, one for her and one for him, and went back into the living room. He sipped the stout. It was stronger than beer. He didn't like it too much.

He waited. The image he had seen a few hours earlier zinged through his brain: Alice bare to the waist, bending over the sink, the heavy globes of her breasts swaying as she washed herself. There was tension inside the killer now as he eagerly anticipated the pleasures of the evening.

A few moments later, Alice reappeared.

"How does this look?" she asked.

"Terrific," he said. And he meant it.

She had changed out of her dinner clothes into some sort of negligee. The ankle-length black gauze didn't hide much of her body, and Floyd was easily aware that she had nothing whatever on underneath. Within the gauzy folds he could make out indistinctly the high hills of her breasts, the fullness of her hips, the white columns of her legs. His pulse began to pound faster.

"I poured some stout for you," he said, grinning.

"Thanks."

She took the glass from him. He saw the heavy globe of a breast within the negligee. Then she turned and crossed the room to close the blinds. He stared at the full round thrusts of her buttocks, half-visible under the negligee. She was all but naked in that outfit, only a couple of millimeters of black silk hiding the fullness of her body from his eyes.

She came back, sat down on the couch, at the opposite end from him. She seemed a really cool cookie, completely poised even in her near-nudity. She had done this plenty of times, Floyd figured.

He stared at her. He could plainly see her breasts, and they were magnificent. The nipples were hidden by the black silk. They sipped their stout in silence.

She said, "How long will you be in New York?"

"I'm leaving tomorrow," he lied.

"Oh. That's too bad. I thought we'd get a chance to get to know each other better."

"It's the breaks," he said.

"Ships that pass in the night, that sort of thing." She shrugged. The shrug made her breasts sway enticingly. "Well, we'll have to make the most of tonight, then, if you go back to the sewer business tomorrow."

She crawled along the couch toward him. She leaned her head against his shoulder. Floyd put his arm around her. He could look right down into the front of her negligee now, from this angle, and he could see the tops of her breasts, tawny and pink-tipped. Excitement tortured him. He brought his hand up and cupped it over her bosom. Her breasts were firm and resilient with youthful tautness that Floyd liked. She had good-sized breasts, but they weren't so large that they looked sloppy.

They kissed.

It was their first kiss, he realized strangely. It seemed as if he had known her for months, but it was really only a few hours, and though he had seen her bare breasts before and had been looking at her in this sheer negligee, their lips had not met until this moment.

He kissed her hard. He wasn't gentle when he kissed, not ever. The hand that was cupped at her breast could detect the quickening of her heartbeat.

When they came up for air, they were both gasping in excitement. She looked at him, eyes misty with awakened lust.

Then she smiled. "We're out of stout," she said. "I'll get some more."

Before he could stop her, she took the empty glasses and darted into the kitchen. Floyd shrugged. Why had she broken the mood like that? They didn't need anything else to drink now. He sat there scowling, listening to her moving around in the kitchen.

Then she returned. Without the negligee.

She carried a glass of stout in each hand, and the negligee was folded over one arm. She stood in the doorway, smiling at him, completely nude.

It made a stunning effect. To have the total nudity of her appear before him in one sudden moment like that was like staring into the sun. For a moment, Floyd was so dazzled by what he saw that the individual details didn't register on him.

But only for a moment.

He eyed her carefully. Her breasts were high and round, without the faintest trace of droop or sag. The nipples were small and bright pink in color.

Her body swept away dizzyingly to the narrowness of her waist. Then there was the magnificent swell of her hips and then the tapering perfection of her legs. Her legs were a little short in proportion to her body, not much. That was her only flaw. She turned, showing him the profile view, and he saw the jutting beauty of her breasts and the voluptuous outcurving swells of her buttocks.

"Well?" she said. "You like?"

"You bet."

"Prettier than the things you find in sewers?"

"You can say that again."

"I won't. Have some stout. You look like you need cooling off."

He took a glass from her. He gulped it down, put it aside. She was half finished with hers. Floyd gently took her glass from her hand and put it next to her empty one. Then he reached for her.

She seemed to flow into his arms. He felt the full globes of her bare breasts flattening out against his chest, the hard points of the nipples against him. He slipped his arms around her, one going around her shoulders, the other moving over her satin-smooth skin to the rounds of her buttocks. He spread his hands out over the firm cool mounds.

Her mouth met his. The kiss was a long one, a fiery, passionate one.

Finally their lips parted. She looked at him, her eyes misty slits of desire. Her full lips, moist and shiny, drew apart in a smile.

"Can I finish my stout now?" she asked huskily.

"If you want to."

"I'll chug-a-lug it," she said.

He watched the rippling fluidity of her body as she turned, picked up her glass, put it to her lips. She tilted her head, making her breasts rise excitingly. The dark liquid vanished from the glass. A moment later she put the glass down, sighing in pleasure.

"That's better," she said. "And now—"

She began to undress him.

Her fingers flew deftly over his clothing, with a skill that indicated plenty of experience. Floyd let her run the show, moving an arm or a leg as she directed, and in a moment or two he was as naked as she was.

"Come here," he said hoarsely.

A second time she flowed into his arms. Now no barrier of clothing stood between them, and Floyd could feel the searing warmth of her nakedness. He brought one hand up to cup her right breast, savoring the weight, the nipple taut against his palm.

She was panting in need now.

She whispered. "Let's not wait. I'm ready. Right now!"

He was ready too. His nerve-ends were raw and tingling. He had to have her. Not five minutes from now, either. Right now.

They fell together, to the carpeted floor.

"Take me!" she cried urgently. "Fast! Be rough with me! Hold me tight."

Floyd was drawn along on the savage tide of her passion. He let himself be drawn to the sleek, tawny softness of her. Her body moved to meet him and he pressed toward her.

"Now!" she cried.

He drove furiously.

She drew him closer. He gasped at the voluptuousness. She wheeled and began to spur him with sharp fingernails. He drove himself, matching the frenzy of her charge, and they galloped toward the heights together.

This was terrific.

This was just what he needed tonight.

Floyd worked his hands underneath to cup the firm flesh of her buttocks. Opening his eyes, he saw the blonde girl's lovely face distorted with passion. Her fingers gripped his hard biceps. Her lips moved wordlessly, and she moaned, and then he heard her say, "Yes, yes, more, *right now!*"

She gasped in a frenzy of fulfillment.

Floyd mounted upward with her, driving higher, gasping as the ecstasy took hold of him, shook him, stunned him. He kissed her violently. She tore away, sucking air into her lungs. He heard her gasp, heard her moan, heard her make a sound like a wild sob, at the height of her passion.

He heard the thunder of ecstasy.

At the same moment she heard the same wild music, and with a weary little sighing sound collapsed limply against the carpet. He lay next to her, breathing hard. After a moment he lifted his head and kissed each pink nipples. They were soft now.

A while afterward, he moved away. He looked at

the nakedness of her. Even now, in his sated state, Floyd responded to her marvelous nudity, the sleekness, the swells of her breasts.

A great little kid, he thought.

Too bad he would never see her again after tonight. But that was his way. He didn't believe in getting involved with women on a long-term basis. Find 'em, love 'em, and then find the next. No matter how nice this one was, there was always another just as good somewhere up the pike, and life was simpler all around if you went looking for that next one all the time instead of stopping when you found something you thought you liked.

A long time later, he left her apartment. She came to the door, nude, to kiss him good-bye.

"Look me up again next time you're in New York," she told him.

"Sure," he said. "You can bet I will."

But don't give big odds, he thought, as he cupped her breasts for the last time, ran his hand down her back to her satiny buttocks, kissed her lightly on the lips, and disappeared from her life.

Gorman took the whip from Marie. The weird ritual began.

She turned her back to him. Her buttocks, outlined by the cruel thongs of the garter-belt, stood out with unnatural fullness. She bent over, giving him a good look at the two soft, tempting hillocks of flesh, which were pulled taut by her stance.

Marie waited. Then Gorman lifted the whip and brought it down lightly to the plump mounds of flesh.

"Harder!" Marie cried, because she knew that was what he wanted her to say. "Hurt me! Punish me! I've been very naughty and I have to be punished!"

"Yes," Gorman muttered thickly. "You have to be punished!"

A second time he flicked the whip over her buttocks, and this time there was a loud sting at the impact. Marie gasped, from the pain. She knew that angry red lines were appearing on the white flesh. But she just had to grin and bear this. At the price he was paying for the privilege of whipping her, this was worth the discomfort.

"Yes!" she cried. "Hit me! Hit me everywhere!"

Gorman raised the whip and struck her across the buttocks again, then the shoulders. She turned to him, eyes growing wild. She was only half play-acting, now. The sting of the whip did something strange to her, turned her on in a way she had never thought possible before Gorman had known her. Marie hated these games, but she couldn't deny that she got genuine thrills out of them.

"My breasts!" she whispered hoarsely. "Whip my breasts, too!"

The whip licked out. The thongs struck across her right breast and the soft flesh quivered, and she hissed in an ecstasy of pain. She dropped to her knees in front of him.

"Master! Master! I deserve my punishment!"

"Take it, then!"

The whip descended on her shoulders, on her breasts, and, as she turned, on her back. Marie scrambled to her feet and he caught her again across the buttocks, then lower, over the backs of her legs. A quick snick of the wrist and the whip punished her in an even more terrifying manner. Marie whimpered.

Gorman was completely carried away in his fantasy, now. He rained a hail of lashes on her. Whipping indiscriminately in every exposed place. She twisted and turned, trying to escape the lash, then she began to flee from him. He followed her through the apartment, pounding after her like a naked satyr, lashing out at her at every turn. He was breathing hard from his exertions. Marie hoped he wouldn't get a heart attack. That would be terrible, if he dropped dead now, before they were married. She wouldn't get a penny.

As they passed through the bedroom, Marie tripped and fell heavily to the floor. She landed on her back. That was part of the routine too. Gorman could not resist. His middle-aged virility was low and flagging, and he needed little tricks like this to keep him amused.

He tossed the whip aside. The game came abruptly to an end as he sank beside her yielding body and with fierce intensity, took her.

It didn't matter to her now that a fat, absurd rich old lecher was holding her. Marie was a naturally passionate girl, and she was so inflamed that any man would serve her need.

They rolled on the floor, her breasts practically in his face.

He seized them, gripping tight.

Then he let go and began to hit her. Not hard, because there wasn't much strength in his flabby body. But hard enough so that she could feel it.

He slapped her breasts, hurting the swollen mounds, back-handed her face, grasped her buttocks and dug his fingers in cruelly. Marie gave a sudden long sigh of ecstasy and redoubled her exertions. She nearly fell as she moved, and reached to hold her in place. They toppled sideways, and in another moment, magic began to happen—first the earthquake of her body, the slow powerful convulsions racking her to the point of unconsciousness, and then his own briefer tremors of joy, accompanied by grunts and ugly rasping wheezing sounds of pleasure.

And then that was over.

They lay on the floor. After a few minutes Marie moved away. His fat, chunky body was drenched with sweat. She stung and ached in the places where his whippings and slappings had hurt her. But he never injured her seriously. It was all play-acting. What bothered her most of all was the costume she had to wear.

She got out of it fast, now that the game was over. She unhooked the cut-out bra and massaged herself along the deep red lines that had been scored into the flesh at the base of her breasts. She unlaced the garter-belt, sighing in relief as the pressure was taken off. Then came the stockings. The tight rubber had hampered the circulation of her legs, and they felt swollen and sticky.

Completely nude, now, Marie caught her breath and unwound after the passionate session.

"I'd better be going, now," Gorman said, getting to his feet.

"Yes. Home to Ethel."

"For the next to last night," he said. "After Saturday, no more Ethel."

Marie grinned. She put her hands over her breasts, squeezing them to soothe the discomfort of the bra she had just taken off. "I can't wait, darling."

"Neither can I."

She helped him to his feet. He dressed quickly. Marie saw him to the door.

It was still early in the evening, not much past ten o'clock. A hot bath, that was the first thing on Marie's schedule. She always felt soiled after these sessions with Howard Gorman. And then—well, she would find ways of amusing herself until it was time to go to sleep. The night was young, and Marie had many friends.

She thought about the killer Gorman had hired, the one who was going to snuff out Ethel Gorman's life come Saturday.

Lee Floyd.

Hotel Ascot.

Marie frowned. The germ of an idea was starting to sprout in her mind.

CHAPTER FIVE

Lee Floyd slept soundly that night. His evening with blonde, blue-eyed Alice had left him relaxed and sleepy. He had gotten back to the hotel around four in the morning, and he was looking forward to a good long snooze.

He didn't get it. At nine o'clock the next morning, energetic drumming on his door woke him. He sprang into wakefulness immediately, even though it meant ripping himself out of a sweet dream of Alice. Floyd was always quick to wake up, no matter how little sleep he had had. In his line of work, you had to be quick about everything you did.

He groped for his silk dressing-gown, found it, began to slip into it.

"Who's there?" he said crisply.

"Acme Messenger Service," an adolescent voice replied. "Are you Mr. Floyd?"

"That's right."

Floyd was grinning as he opened the door. Old man Gorman had come through with Installment Number One then, right on the button.

The delivery boy was holding a bulky manila envelope. He pushed a pad toward Floyd and said, "Sign here." Floyd signed. The kid handed him the manila envelope and started to leave.

"Hold on a second," Floyd said. He turned, picked a quarter off his dresser, and handed it to the delivery boy. "Here," he said. "Go out and get drunk."

The kid disappeared. Floyd closed the door and locked it. He put the packet on the desk and stared at it. It was thick, well packed, with a seal on it. Gorman obviously wasn't a man who sent money around in any old slipshod way, Floyd thought.

He had to work hard to rip the packet open. There was an inner package too, sealed with some kind of reinforced tape that was tough work to open. Floyd fought his way through it, ripped the inner wrapper open.

He saw green.

Lots and lots of the long green.

There were three bundles of bills, each still bearing its bank wrapper of manila paper. Floyd broke the wrappers and counted out the bills. There were ten hundred-dollar bills, twenty fifty-buck bills, and twenty-five twenties.

Grand total, twenty-five hundred smackers.

Floyd gave the bills a good checking-out. They were neat and clean, but they weren't brand new. That was good. Brand new bills would have consecutive serial numbers, and that could pose problems. On close inspection, none of the bills appeared to bear any suspicious markings. Not that Floyd was seriously worried about a double-cross on Gorman's part; the fat executive just didn't seem to be that type. Maybe he was capable of having his wife murdered, but he didn't look like the kind of guy who would take any risks trying to cross up a hired killer. Even so, Floyd figured, it paid to be over-cautious. In this and in everything.

The bills added up into a pretty thick wad. Floyd stacked them neatly and slipped them into the inner pocket of his billfold, where they made a healthy-looking bulge. It was the kind of bulge he liked. Once the money was put away he gathered up the wrappers that had contained it, ripped them into small shreds, and carefully stuffed the shreds into the wastebasket.

Okay, he thought. That was fifty per cent of the loot, cash on the barrelhead. So far, so good.

He wriggled out of his dressing-gown and went

into the bathroom to take a shower. A long empty day stretched ahead of him, and at least the sun was shining today. He wondered what he'd do. Wander around town, see a movie, maybe pick up another girl. It was a temptation, of course, to go back to Alice's place and tell her that he was staying in town another day. But even though the idea of getting into the sack with her was agreeable enough, Floyd wanted to avoid turning a one-night stand into a romance. That could lead to trouble—especially if she got interested enough in civil engineering to find out a little about it, and ask him any embarrassing questions.

Floyd dressed slowly. At quarter after ten the telephone rang. Floyd picked it up.

"Hello?"

He heard Gorman's oddly high-pitched voice say, "Is that you, Floyd?"

"It isn't Santa Claus."

"Did the package—"

"Yeah, it got here all right," Floyd said. "They were nice, crisp ones. You print them yourself?"

Gorman chuckled with phony joviality. "Heh-heh! Very funny!"

"Yeah."

"I've got the second batch all ready for you, Floyd. They'll be delivered to you at the same time tomorrow morning, at your hotel room. And then my end of the obligation will be fulfilled."

"I'll take care of this end of it tomorrow night," Floyd told him in a soft voice. "Don't you worry about that. Just don't you worry any."

"I can't wait," said Gorman. "I saw Marie last night and she looked lovelier than ever. And passionate. Just a few more days, I keep telling myself, and—well, you know how it is."

Yeah, Floyd thought. *I know exactly how it is, Mr. Gorman.*

Out loud he said, "Tomorrow night all your troubles will be over, believe me. Just get the cash here on time and leave the rest for me to take care of."

He hung up.

He began to take clothes out. He was almost finished dressing when the telephone rang again. What now, he wondered? Gorman calling back to bother him some more?

Floyd frowned, rose cautiously, and looked around the room. Everything looked all right. He wondered if the line might have been tapped. No, he decided. Not a chance of it. He picked up the receiver.

"Hello?"

"Mr. Floyd? Are you alone?"

It was a woman's voice, low, breathy. Floyd went tense. He was off balance now. Somebody he didn't know knew his name. It wasn't Alice's voice, but she didn't know his real name, anyway. And he couldn't imagine another woman who might be calling him here. He was uneasy, not knowing where to go from here. He didn't like it when an element of doubt figured into his operations.

"Who's this?" he said.

"A friend. I wanted to know—is Howard Gorman with you?"

Floyd chewed his lower lip. After a pause he said, "Mr. Gorman isn't here. Did you want to see him?"

"Not exactly. Not now, that is. You're the one I want to see, but it would be awkward if Howard was with you. Do you mind if I come up? I'm calling from the hotel lobby."

Again Floyd paused. After a moment's thought he

said, "Do you want to tell me what you want to see me about? Or who you are?"

"I can't very well talk about it on the phone," the girl said. "But maybe you know me by name. My name's Marie. Can I come up?"

Marie?

Gorman's girl friend Marie?

"Yeah," Floyd said. "Yeah. Come on up."

Three or four minutes later somebody knocked twice, very gently, on the door of Floyd's room. He kept calm as he went to open it.

Marie stood there. She was a surprise.

She was a tall girl, standing about five feet six or so, which brought her almost to the level of Floyd's compact five feet eight. She wore a light green jacket that was thrown open over a low-cut red dress. High, firm breasts were on display in the scoop of her neckline, taut upthrust mounds of flesh that looked very good, even this early in the morning.

She wasn't anything like the painted floozie that Floyd had been picturing her as. She had class and charm. Surveying her panther-like grace as she stood in the hall, the killer could see that this was indeed a woman that might provoke a mild-mannered type like Howard Gorman into wanting to kill his wife. Yes. She was pretty spectacular, to put it gently. Floyd was impressed.

He found his tongue and said, "Won't you come in?"

"Thank you."

She stepped into the room, and Floyd clicked the door shut. It was a small hotel room, and this was a lot of woman to have in it. Floyd's blood surged. He still didn't have the foggiest idea what she might want with him.

Easily, casually, she slid out of her jacket, revealing bare shoulders and smooth white arms. It was an expensive dress that she was wearing, and it did things to her figure that Floyd didn't find hard to appreciate. Her stunning bust line was molded to maximum effect. The dress clung eye-catchingly to the contours of her hips and buttocks. Probably, Floyd thought, the dress was a gift from Howard Gorman.

She said, "Do you know who I am?"

"Howard Gorman's girl friend."

She nodded. "That's right. I saw Howard last night. He told me that he had had lunch with you yesterday. I found out from him where you were staying, in case you were wondering how I reached you."

"I was."

"Howard isn't supposed to visit you here today for any reason, is he?"

"No," Floyd said. "He isn't. I had a telephone call from him about fifteen minutes ago, but he isn't going to be over here."

"I was so worried I'd bump into him," Marie said. "I didn't want him to see me come up here. That would have really caused a mess."

She lowered herself into a chair, crossing her legs languidly. The skirt rode up high, above her knees. She didn't pull it down. Floyd's lips felt dry. He studied the long legs, the hips, the shoulders, the generous abundance of bosom.

This was a woman who looked good in clothes, he thought.

But Floyd was willing to bet she'd look even better without them. Good old Howard had really struck oil, Floyd thought. Yeah.

"You care for a drink?" Floyd said.

"I'd rather stay here and talk."

"I got a bottle here," he said. He pulled out the bourbon. "No mix, but you can have it with water if you like."

She nodded at the sight of the bourbon bottle. "I'll have it straight," she said.

He grinned at her and poured a shot into a water glass and handed it to her. A point in her favor, he figured. Floyd liked a girl who drank her liquor straight, without messing it up with ice cubes or club soda or any other trimmings.

She held the glass expectantly, as if waiting for him to pour some for himself. When he didn't, she said, "What's the matter with you? Not having any?"

"No. Go ahead," he said. "I don't drink. Bad for the reflexes. Beer and some wine, that's all I touch."

She smiled knowingly and put the glass to her lips. She belted it down in two gulps. Pretty good drinking for half past ten in the morning, Floyd thought.

"More?" he said.

"Not just now." She eyed him closely. "Did you and Howard reach any sort of agreement?"

"Yes," he said. "But you had my price wrong."

"Three thousand?"

"No. Five."

"I heard three."

"You heard wrong," he said.

Marie shrugged. The shrug made her breasts dance around and practically fall out of her neckline. It was quite a sight.

"My apologies," she said. "I got the info through the grapevine. Everyone's pretty vague about things like that, you know."

"Yeah. I know."

"But tell me: did Howard agree to pay you the higher price?"

Floyd nodded. "Yeah," he said. "We have a contract." *And whatever he's paying, it's worth it to get a clear path to something that looks like you,* Floyd added silently.

"Good," she said. "When is the blessed event scheduled to take place?"

"That's my business."

"You don't need to keep any secrets from me. I helped to set this deal up, you know,"

He shrugged. "It's going to be Saturday night. I'll be at Gorman's at midnight."

Marie smiled. "It's about time the old witch died. You don't know how it's been, us having to slink around like thieves all the time, afraid that someone will see us and tell Ethel. Howard's very afraid of that, you know. He always hated the possibility that there might be some sort of a scandal. But soon it'll be all over, won't it?"

"Yeah," Floyd said. "Soon enough."

"I can't wait."

"How come Howard just doesn't get a divorce, if he's afraid of trouble?"

"He doesn't want to drag his wife through the courts. He doesn't have any grounds on her, and that means he'd have to give *her* grounds and talk her into suing. This way is better for business, Howard thinks. Executives who get divorced and then marry younger women are—well, looked down on."

"I get it."

"A violent death is more shocking, but socially it's more acceptable."

Floyd nodded distantly. He was surveying the girl's smooth grace, her poise and seductive loveliness, as she sat with her legs crossed in his armchair. She was a fabulous creature. Alice, last night, had been a good kid with a great body, but she was just an old spinster next to this one. Floyd was thinking, *What a waste to let Howard Gorman have a chick like this. What a stinking waste.*

The thought annoyed him. Temptation was a troublesome thing. Floyd had conducted his business, up to now, just that way—purely as a business. Stopping to dally with the client's girl friend was against business ethics. Also a risky complication, Floyd thought.

But still, this was quite a woman. She was enough woman so that it might justify a slight variation from his usual business procedure.

Floyd said softly, "You didn't just come up here to pass the time of day, Marie. What's the scoop?"

She said, "Howard's paying you five thousand dollars to rid himself of Ethel. I've got a business proposition for you too."

Floyd blinked, quick, on-off. "What kind of proposition?"

"I want a man killed," she said. "I understand that that's your specialty. He's a fat fiftyish sort of businessman. I think you can guess the one I mean."

He narrowed his eyes in surprise. What he had just heard astonished him. And the words had dropped so coolly from her lovely red lips, too. Even though he was accustomed to dealing with people who had murder on their minds, he didn't quite expect anything as cold-blooded as this.

But he recovered quickly and nodded as if it didn't matter at all.

"I think I know who you mean."

"Would you take on the job?"

"It depends," he said. "It's my business, after all, doing jobs like that. But it depends."

"On what?"

"On a lot of things. Keep talking and fill me in on

all this."

"It's pretty simple." she said. "I want you to remove him. I'm hiring you."

"I'm expensive."

"That's one of the things I wanted to discuss with you. The fee. I'd prefer not to pay you in cash. I'd rather offer something else than money to pay your price."

"What?" he asked

"Me," she said.

CHAPTER SIX

The room suddenly became very quiet. Marie was breathing hard, her proud breasts climbing a few inches with each sharp intake of air. Floyd kept waiting for her nipples to pop into view. He stood there, saying nothing until the drumming in his ears stopped.

He led a nice, uncomplicated kind of life, doing his jobs, getting paid his money. And now along came Marie promising all sorts of complications.

"Let's backtrack a little," he said. "You want to get rid of Howard?"

"I hate his stinking guts!" The lovely face suddenly became an ugly mask hiding some deeper ugliness. "You know why he says he wants me? He wants to prove that he's still a man, still got something a woman might want. But he's no lover. It would make you throw up if I told you what kind of perverted things he makes me do so he can enjoy himself."

Floyd was quiet. The details of Howard Gorman's love life didn't interest him.

Marie went on, "All he's got that I'm interested in is money. Period. When I go to bed with him he disgusts me. You think I want to be some rich man's plaything?"

"Well?"

"I'm going to get him to write a new will tonight, naming me. I'll point out to him that you never know what might happen to you, and if he died suddenly before I was his wife, Ethel would get everything. Or if he dropped dead after Ethel died, the state would grab it all. He doesn't have any children, and I know he doesn't want Ethel to get his money. Or the government, for that matter."

"You think you can get him to write a new will just like that?"

"I know I can." An undercurrent of excitement throbbed in Marie's deep voice as she said huskily, "Okay. So a killer comes to town to get rid of Ethel. Why not get rid of Howard, too? I get all his money, and ..."

"And what?"

She flicked her tongue out over her full red lips. "You're just like I pictured you," she said. "Thin and hard and cold, and all death. You're what I want. You and me and the late Howard Gorman's bank account. We'll go places, the three of us!"

Floyd was rocked by the proposal. He had seen this coming, but now that it was out in the open it shook him. Marie ... his? This flawless, sensual, superb hunk of woman? All his? For keeps?

He had never let himself take on a permanent mistress. Partly because in his business it didn't make any sense to snarl yourself up with a woman, but also because he hadn't found anyone really worth his while on a long-term basis. But this Marie was something different. She was the most beautiful girl he had ever seen. And she'd be his on a platinum platter, with all of Howard Gorman's money. With Gorman's dough, they could take a long trip to nowhere and still have plenty left.

A muscle flickered in Floyd's cheek. He took a step closer toward her. She looked up at him, her eyes glowing with the promise of thrills.

He put on hand on her bare shoulder.

"Is it a deal?" she asked, getting to her feet.

Her eyes were almost on a level with his when she stood up. So were her lips.

He thought of her naked in his bed five minutes from now. He thought how he would like to kiss her bare breasts and have her soft skin against him.

He said, "It's a deal."

He grabbed her roughly. Her warmth spread against his body. His hand cupped over the upper half of one of her nearly bare breasts. The flesh was good against his fingers. She wriggled sensuously, her mouth was warm against his.

He started to move her toward the bed. Then suddenly she pulled away. Her breath was hard. Her lipstick was smeared, her dress awry.

"Well?" he asked. "What's wrong? We got a deal. We got to make it official."

She shook her head. "Not now. Not here."

"Baby, that's called teasing."

"I can't help it, Lee. We'll make it official a little later."

"Why not now?"

"I've got to go. I've got to see somebody else, and I don't want to be late."

"That's pretty thin."

"I'm sorry," Marie said. "Believe me, I want you, but I don't want a quickie. That would spoil everything. Our first time ought to be something fancier."

"Yeah. I guess."

"Right now I feel rushed. I feel the pressure of this appointment. I'll come back later and I'll spend all night with you. That's the right way to begin. Now I've only got maybe ten minutes. Later we'll have all the time in the world. Okay?"

"When will you come back here?"

Marie looked at her watch. "I'm meeting Howard for dinner at half past five. Ethel thinks it's an important business conference. He loved me last night, so he won't want to again, I hope." An expression of disgust crossed her face. "Thank God *that'll* be over soon. Unless he gets into an amorous mood, Howard will probably be going home to Ethel around eight, nine o'clock. I could be here, say, by half past nine. How's that?"

"For all night?"

"Yes."

"Suppose he wants to love you?" Floyd asked. "You'll come here after *him?*"

"Don't worry," Marie said throatily. "I'll give him a song-and-dance. I'll tell him that I don't feel well. I'll manage."

"Okay. See you around half past nine, then. If they ask any questions in the lobby, just tell them that you're my sister."

She grinned. Then she moved toward him for a second kiss. Her body was soft and yielding against his. He held her tight, savoring the touch of her against him. He put his hands on her breasts again. The skin was like fine satin.

"There," she said, when they broke apart. "That ought to hold you till tonight."

Marie rode down in the elevator with the touch of Lee Floyd's kiss still on her lips. She was in a strange, tense mood. He was a tough little man, she thought. Just the way a killer ought to be.

But he obviously wanted her. The disappointment on his face when she said she had to leave was clear and unmistakable.

Well, there wasn't any time now. Marie wanted to get over to Dolores' place for a little Lesbo fun. She'd be back at the Ascot tonight, and then Lee Floyd could have his fun. Marie was looking forward to it. She figured that the lean little man would be an exciting lover. He had that kind of strange power coiled up in him.

She hurried over to Dolores' place.

It was still before noon when Marie got there. She had to ring the bell three times. Finally there was some sleepy response from within, and then the door opened. Dolores stood there, her dark hair tousled and bedraggled.

"Morning," Marie said.

"Is it?" Dolores said.

Marie grinned and stepped inside. Dolores was nude. Marie's body was tingling with the excitement that Lee Floyd had aroused, and the sight of Dolores' curving buttocks and breasts spurred her to new stimulation.

"It's close to afternoon," Marie said. "I've been up for hours. You'd be surprised at some of the things I've been doing this morning."

"I didn't get to bed till six," Dolores said. "I picked up this wonderful guy, this advertising man from Connecticut. He just got divorced, and he's looking for a girl friend, and, well, we had ourselves a ball."

"What would Paul say?"

"Who's going to tell him? You cheat on Howard, don't you?"

"With you."

"I mean with other men."

"Sometimes," Marie said. "I guess you haven't had breakfast yet."

"You're changing the subject. But I haven't. Look, make yourself comfortable. I want to go take a shower. You put some coffee up, or something."

Dolores disappeared into the bathroom, her bare buttocks switching provocatively from side to side. Marie glanced after her. Then she took her dress off. She had deliberately donned a lurid dress that morning for the benefit of Lee Floyd, but it wasn't her idea of usual midday clothing. The push'em-up bra was an uncomfortable thing to wear, though it certainly made a striking effect. She freed herself of that. All she wore now was her stockings and panties and garter-belt. That was about right, she thought.

She put some coffee up, rummaged in the refrigerator, got some toast going for Dolores' breakfast and some sandwiches for her own lunch. A short while later, Dolores came out of the shower, looking wide awake, her body pink and glistening, her nipples tall and hard.

They had breakfast, and lunch, and they talked. It was just idle chitter-chatter. Marie didn't dare tell Dolores what was in the wind. Dolores was a good kid, but there was no sense bringing her into a murder conspiracy. She was just somebody to go to bed with when the mood struck.

After lunch, Dolores said, "Shall we?"

"Why not?"

They walked arm in arm into the bedroom.

"You're still all dressed up," Dolores said.

"You can take care of that."

"Don't think I won't," she said.

She rolled Marie's panties down, inch by inch over her waist and legs, and off. Marie stepped out of the filmy garment.

Dolores knelt in front of her. She placed her hands on the cool cheeks of Marie's bottom, and leaned her face forward to the red-haired girl's firm, taut waist. For a long moment the caress continued. Marie looked down, saw the heavy globes of Dolores' bare breasts swaying, and delighted in the intense sensations of pleasure.

Dolores glanced up. Her eyes were shining with delight. "You are good," she said, panting.

"Hurry up and finish undressing me, then."

"Sure. Sure."

Nimbly, Dolores unclipped Marie's garters and peeled her stockings away. The garter-belt followed. Now not a stitch of clothing hid either girl's body.

Dolores rose. She became a wildcat, pulling Marie to the bed, turning to her, grasping, squeezing, kissing. She seized every part of Marie's body in turn, paying homage with eager lips.

Marie knew the fires of her own passions were rising to an uncontrollable level.

She let herself be caught in the fervor of the other girl's lust. Her body trembled. Her breasts swelled, her nipples rose and throbbed, and there was a sunburst of warmth over her.

Desire, raw and elemental, took complete hold of her.

Marie grabbed at Dolores' heavy, swollen breasts. She gripped them, holding so tightly that Dolores gasped in mingled pleasure and pain. She sought out Dolores' soft lips and found them.

Body teased soft, feminine, voluptuously abundant body.

Passions mounted.

Breast touched and teased breast.

Hands clawed at firm fleshy hips. Lustful lips caressed avidly.

"Marie!" Dolores cried. "Marie, Marie!"

"Dolores!"

"This is so sweet. Oh ... so good."

"Yes!"

"Oh, you are so good to me!"

"Hold me! Hold me!"

"I am."

"Tighter."

"I'm trying, Marie."

"Oh, squeeze me dearest!"

"Like this, baby?"

"Yes!"

"And this?"

"Oh, yes!"

"Are you getting there, Marie?"

"A mile a minute," Marie gasped. "Here. Let me put my hand—"

"Yes," Dolores panted. "Oh, yes, baby!"

"I'll give you more."

"All you have."

"Yes!"

"Yes!"

"*Yes!*"

Sensation dissolved into swirling flames. Lust was a volcano within Marie's sweating body. Tense and distended, the two girls grappled desires, a struggle of lust, a combat of pounding ecstasies.

Together they went shooting upward through the outer reaches of the stratosphere.

Breaking through, heading for distant galaxies.

Then came the blinding explosion of shared passion, the single coruscating instant of fulfillment, the mutual sunburst of joy.

And then began the long, slow descent to reality once again. They lay together, tired and sweaty and happy, purged for the moment of all needs, and Marie felt tender hands cupping her breasts, and soft lips grazing her skin, and she smiled, and ran her hands gently through Dolores' lustrous dark hair, and closed her eyes, and let a blissful tide or relaxation steal steadily over her.

Tomorrow, Marie thought.

Tomorrow was the big day.

Ethel Gorman would be dead tomorrow. And maybe Howard Gorman would be dead too. Check and checkmate for the Gormans. And all that nice money would drop into Marie's waiting hands. How much? She didn't know, but it was well up there in six figures, she was sure of that. At least half a million bucks, Marie figured, and maybe a lot more.

What could you do with half a million bucks?

Plenty, Marie thought.

You could buy yourself a shiny little Jaguar with about six thousand of it. You could have a vacation in the Caribbean for another thousand or two. A pearl necklace—well, say five hundred. Dior gowns. Enough Joy and Chanel to take baths in.

And lots, lots else. Marie did some quick arithmetic. You could invest half a million bucks at six per cent and it would give you thirty thousand cookies a year. That was six hundred bucks a week, more or less, without ever dipping into your capital. Marie could figure out a lot of interesting things to do with six hundred dollars a week. And there was always the chance, she knew, that good old Howard-daddy was worth a lot more.

Tomorrow, she thought, would tell the tale.

Marie smiled. She cuddled against her pal Dolores.

"You know something?" Marie asked.

"What?"

"It's a good life," Marie said. "If you know how to get what you want."

It was quarter past five. Time to leave the office for his date with Marie. Howard Gorman was full of tension and apprehension.

One more day, he thought, and then Ethel was finished. Floyd would take care of her. It was strange to think that the old bat would be dead. Gorman almost regretted having decided to hire a killer to finish off his wife. But only almost.

Who would have known, that day thirty years or so back when he proposed to Ethel, that it would end up with murder?

She had been a good-looking girl back then. Not really beautiful—Ethel had never been beautiful—but she had been attractive enough, with a slender body, nice legs, a good pair of breasts. Of course, breasts hadn't really been fashionable back then. It was all the rage to make yourself look flat-chested, but Gorman had always liked a woman with boobs, fashion or no fashion, and Ethel had had a pretty pair. He had thought he loved her.

He had been pretty passionate, too. He could remember their wedding night. Ethel had been a virgin. Virginity had been fashionable too, back then. They had gone to a hotel, and he had tactfully undressed in the bathroom, and when he came out Ethel had her nightgown on, and he turned off the light and got into bed with her, and gently took the nightgown off, and felt the smoothness of her body, caressed her firm young breasts, heard her panting in anticipation.

"Be gentle," she whispered.

Then he took her. She didn't respond, of course. It wasn't really the proper thing back then for a woman to seem too passionate in bed, except for a prostitute. And Ethel was inexperienced, anyway. But she let him have her, and so they began their marriage, and gradually she got older and flabbier, and then along came Marie.

And so Ethel had to die. It was as simple as that. Gorman had nothing personal against his wife, but she stood in the way of his pleasure, and at his age he couldn't afford to wait for her to kick off naturally.

Marie was too seductive a creature to resist. Gorman would do anything for Marie.

Anything.

He hurried over to the restaurant where they were meeting for dinner. Gorman didn't intend to go to bed with Marie tonight. He was fifty-five, after all. A man had to pace himself when he got past fifty. Last night had been enough for him for a few days. All that frenzied whipping, running around the apartment after her, falling on her and taking her— that had been enough exertion for the time being. They would make love again in a few days, Gorman figured—to celebrate his new freedom.

Marie wasn't at the restaurant yet when Gorman' got there. He hadn't really expected her to be. Punctuality wasn't one of Marie's strong points. Gorman took a seat at the bar and had a martini while he waited.

She showed up ten minutes late. She looked absolutely gorgeous, in her low-cut dress with the gleaming tops of her breasts dazzlingly displayed. Gorman wheeled round from his bar stool and went to her.

"Darling," he said, taking her hand.

"Hello, Howard. Waiting long?"

"A minute or two. You look so lovely today!"

She smiled. "Thank you, Howard. That's very kind of you to say."

They went to the table that Gorman had reserved. It was still too early to have dinner, so he ordered another martini for himself. Marie had a manhattan. Gorman stared across the table at her as though she were some dream-vision that was likely to fade away if he took his attention away from her for a moment.

"Tomorrow," he murmured. "Tomorrow's the big day."

"I can't wait."

"Neither can I."

She pursed her lips solemnly. "But I've been thinking about something very serious, Howard. What if something happened to you before we were married?"

"What could happen?"

"I don't mean to be a jinx," she said. "But you've got to face the practical realities. I mean, let's look at them cold-bloodedly."

"All right," he said, puzzled. "Let's."

"You're not a young man. I know your health is good, but even so, things unexpectedly happen. You overexert yourself sometimes. Like last night. You were so frisky last night that I thought you might have an attack."

"My heart's perfectly sound, Marie."

"For a man your age. Yes. But things happen suddenly. What I'm getting at is this, Howard. If you died tonight, or tomorrow, or any time in the next couple of months before it was proper for us to get married, who would inherit your estate? You've got no heirs except ..."

"Except Ethel," he said. "I hadn't really thought about that. If Ethel's gone ..."

"And Ethel *will* be gone."

He nodded. "It would all be grabbed by the government. Or go to charity. I've left myself wide open and left you out in the cold."

"It can be fixed," Marie said.

Gorman nodded. Marie had a point. It was a little tactless of her to bring it up, but he couldn't deny that she made sense. According to his existing will, Ethel was his sole heir, except for a few minor charitable bequests. Marie would get nothing if he happened to die before their marriage. That made absolutely no sense. He wanted Marie to get the benefit of her association with him, if anything happened to him. And he had to be level-headed about the possibilities. Once you get to a certain age, it can happen in the twinkling of an eye.

He said, "I'll take care of it this very evening," he said. "I'll draw up a new will before we leave the restaurant. They'll give us some blank paper. Then we'll get it notarized and I'll give you a copy of it."

"That's wise, Howard."

"I'm glad you pointed this out to me," he said. "I just didn't think about wills. I've gone through so much of my life thinking that Ethel was going to be my only beneficiary, you see."

"That's all going to change now, darling."

"Yes," he said. "It's going to change very soon."

CHAPTER SEVEN

For Floyd, the day had been crawling along at a torturing pace. He had gone down to the hotel coffee shop for breakfast right after Marie had left him, and then he returned to his room instead of going out for a walk. He felt tense and jumpy in the changed situation. He kept going over Marie's conversation with him, again and again and again, replaying every bit of it in his mind, including the two clinches, including the touch of her lips, including the feel of her warm smooth breasts to his hands.

She was coming back to see him tonight, she had said. He couldn't wait. Although he was usually a patient man, able to bide his time to achieve his ends, right now Floyd was a mass of impatience.

He oiled the .38 two or three times, played Poker Solitaire until it sickened him and he swept the cards into a scrambled heap, then shut his eyes and sprawled out on the bed, seeing Marie on the screen of his closed eyelids.

Marie.

He didn't even know the damned girl's last name, he realized. But that didn't matter much. He knew how she was built and how she kissed. And a little later today he would find out how she loved, unless she had only been playing games with him and wasn't planning to come back. And somehow he doubted that.

He thought about her and Gorman. How had such a fat slob picked up such a chick, anyway? Maybe Gorman had met her at some stag dinner, or had gotten her through a call girl service. Floyd didn't know how she had earned her keep before she had met Gorman. Gorman had told him that she had once danced at a big New York night club, but that wasn't necessarily the truth. Maybe she had been a stripper, or a streetwalker, or a nude girlie-mag model, or something like that.

She wasn't any virgin, that was for sure. But that didn't bother Floyd. He wasn't any choir boy.

He could see the pattern of Gorman's love affair: the aging, potbellied executive falling head-over-heels in love with the shrewd cookie with the lovely fabulous torso. Maybe Marie had taken Gorman to bed a couple of times and had talked him into thinking that he was the greatest thing yet unleashed on the female sex. A girl like Marie would know how to play on a man's masculine vanity, to twist him around her little finger.

And then would follow months of slipping her dough on the sly, of seeing her at odd moments stolen from business or from his wife, of dreaming about her luscious body, and eventually of becoming willing to kill to have her. So then Gorman hires an out-of-town thug named Lee Floyd to finish off Mrs. Gorman, who had ceased to hold any interest for her husband some time in 1937.

Nice. Yeah, very nice.

And then old Gorman would have the breasty redhead all to himself for the rest of his days. What he didn't know was what a short time the rest of his days would amount to, Floyd thought.

Gorman simply hadn't stopped to figure that there might be someone else willing to kill for Marie.

Nor had it occurred to him that Marie might already be looking past her pudgy boy friend to somebody a little younger, a little better-looking, a little more virile in the virility department.

Gorman was just a natural-born patsy, Floyd figured. Probably the old guy spent all his time thinking about Marie, when he ought to be thinking about other things. Marie was his whole world. Maybe he was so nutty about her that he even hired a tail to make sure she was faithful to him. Floyd made a mental note to keep an eye open for anything like that. But if he thought she loved him, he would have another think or three coming tomorrow night. Gorman was nothing but a walking bank account for Marie, no more. He'd be in for a real shock when Floyd gunned him down.

And then Marie would belong to Lee Floyd.

Floyd's fingers started to tremble at that thought, but he managed to calm them down quick enough. Floyd had tremendous control over his nerves. Except for the nerve that was aching for Marie.

She was quite a female. And that speech of hers was too pat to be a spur-of-the-moment thing. Probably she had been planning all along to have the hired killer knock off Gorman too. Whoever had first put her on Floyd's trail probably had described him to her, and she must have decided right then and there what she was going to do.

Floyd paced the hotel room floor. It was one o'clock, now. Eight and a half hours more before Marie returned to him.

And two days after that Mr. and Mrs. Howard Gorman would both be dead, and Marie would be the property of Lee Floyd. That was a lot better a deal than he had been figuring on when he hopped the eastward bus from Cleveland.

Around half past three Floyd got tired of counting the feet and inches on the floor of his room. He went downstairs to the hotel lobby, bought himself a newspaper and a couple of magazines, and went into the coffee shop to have a late lunch.

He munched a hamburger and looked through the

paper. Not much news there. The magazines were pretty dull too. He left them lying on his table and went outside into the busy street.

The bright sunlight of earlier in the day had given way now to a kind of thick haze that was almost like smog. It lay over the city, muggy, dank, swampy, blanketing it smotheringly. Prelude to death, Floyd thought. People walked hurriedly through the haze, scurrying on earnestly to special places of their own.

He strolled casually down Park Avenue. As he walked, he thought back over the jobs he had pulled since getting into his present profession. Eleven killings altogether, carried out from Maine to California, all done with the same neat finesse he liked to think was the Lee Floyd trademark. And murders number twelve and thirteen in the series would be coming up tomorrow night. Yeah. And then Marie.

Floyd had a passport. He had taken it out two years ago, part of his general foresight. He kept it handy, just in case. And this was a case. Marie would go to Bermuda, exactly as Gorman had planned, only she would meet Lee Floyd instead of Howard Gorman. Gorman was going to be dead by the time Marie got to Bermuda. And when they got tired of Bermuda, there was Jamaica, Venezuela, Rio, the Riviera, the whole stinking world.

If he played it well, Gorman's money would never run out at all. They could probably live like lords just spending the income from the money, not touching the principal at all. Of course, Floyd knew, he would have to stay well in the background until the will was cleared, but he didn't expect much trouble there. People would obviously know that Marie had cashed in because she was Gorman's mistress, but things like that happened all the time, and nobody could prevent her from collecting the dough. There were no troublesome relatives to contest the will.

Floyd smiled. This was going to be his biggest job, in more ways than one.

He wandered down Park Avenue past all the glass skyscrapers to 48th Street, then turned west and ambled back up Madison, watching the hurrying New Yorkers racing by. There were lots of pretty girls, lovely as poems in their summer dresses. Skirts were short this year. Strolling along, Floyd studied the bobbling bosoms, the flashing legs. Lots and lots of fine girls here on Manhattan's East Side. Floyd didn't doubt that he could make a pickup just as easily today as he had snared Alice yesterday. But he didn't want to. He wanted to save himself for Marie.

It was five o'clock, now. Pretty soon, he thought. Marie and Howard Gorman would be meeting at some restaurant for dinner and a discussion of Gorman's will, while Ethel wondered how her husband's latest "business conference" was turning out.

Poor Ethel.

Poor Howard, Floyd thought.

He invested a dollar eighty in a movie, and killed a couple of hours in the dark. It was a wild movie, a Swedish job about two girls who go to a strange country and get into some peculiar adventures. There were some pretty dazzling shots of bare breasts and even a bare hip shot that had somehow slipped by the censors. You needed quick eyes to see, because the shot was only on quicker eyes than Lee Floyd's.

The steamy, torrid picture left him keyed up eager for love. He left the theater a little past seven o'clock with time to kill. This was always the roughest part of a job, the wasting of time before and after. It didn't look good to arrive in town and leave, all the same day as you did the job. You never could tell who might be watching your comings and goings.

Floyd's technique was to show up early and leave late, sticking around a couple of days after doing the job instead of skiing out of town right away. That took patience and a certain amount of guts. Usually, Floyd had all the patience in the world. But now, with Marie in the picture, it wasn't easy to keep waiting. He couldn't help remembering that clinging embrace this morning, and her soft, husky-voiced promise of more to come later.

He had a snack at a pizza stand. About half past eight, he returned to his hotel room, and sat down to wait for Marie to arrive.

Twenty to ten. Floyd realized that he'd been watching the second hand of his wristwatch swing round and round the dial for more than an hour, just sitting there almost hypnotized letting the time tick away. Twenty to ten.

And then there came the light double knock on the door of his room.

Floyd was out of his chair and over to the door in one big bound. He quickly unlocked the door and grabbed the handle. Then he recovered his usual caution and opened the door just a crack.

Enough to show Marie standing outside.

He grinned at her. She slid through the half-opened door and into his arms. Her full, voluptuous body was quite an armful. Her mouth went to his. He kissed down hard and hungrily. He held her for a long moment, her body undulating excitingly. Then he released her and locked the door again.

She said, "I told the night clerk I was your maiden aunt from Kankakee. He let me go up to visit you, but he said I shouldn't stay here more than about five or six hours tops."

"That ought to be enough," Floyd said.

He looked at her. She had changed her dress since this morning, but it hadn't been to get into something more chaste. Now she wore a clinging gold-lame thing that seemed to begin around the vicinity of her navel and sweep shiningly downward. The full globes of her breasts were on display like jewels in a fine jewel-case, thrust upward by some magical kind of brassiere that hid her only as far as the nipple line. He could almost make out the first rosy curve of the aureole rising into view.

She moved slowly across the room, with cat-grace, and put her wrap down. She was quite a sight. The rear view was just as spectacular as the front, with the dress molding the contours clearly and explicitly. It was the kind of dress a girl could probably get arrested for wearing in some of the small Middle Western towns.

"How was your dinner date with Howard?" Floyd asked.

"Oh, tolerable, tolerable."

"You talk about the will?"

"I did more than talk about it," she said. "I got him to write a new one right in front of me. We got it witnessed and notarized and everything."

"Hey, that's pretty good work."

"I thought so too. You want to see it?"

"Sure," he said.

She picked up her tiny purse and drew out a folded sheet of white paper. Floyd took it from her. The document wasn't a very elaborate one. It was headed CODICIL, and simply said, "In the event that my wife Ethel F. Gorman should predecease me, the share of my estate that was to have gone to her is now to be left to Miss Marie Caldwell. All other bequests as specified in my earlier will are to remain as designated therein." It was signed and dated, and witnessed, and there was a notary's stamp at the bottom.

"I've got a copy and he's got a copy," Marie said. "Everything nice and official."

"Yeah," Floyd said. He handed the document back to her. "You know, until I read this, I didn't even know your last name? Caldwell. Marie Caldwell."

"Now you know," Marie said. She kissed the piece of paper and put it back in her purse.

"He didn't want to make love tonight, did he?" Floyd asked.

"No. I told you he wouldn't. He was still all tuckered out from yesterday. I would have told him I was sick, if he tried to go home with me, though. It would have been true, too. I am sick of him!"

Floyd smiled. He slipped up behind her and rubbed his hands along her soft bare shoulders, then down her back. The clinging dress was cut even more deeply in back than in front. Floyd felt the firm muscles rippling in her shoulders. His hands went lower. Then they slid around to the front of her body. He cupped them to the full, ripe mounds of her breasts.

Suddenly Marie turned and pressed herself savagely against him, her body gluing itself to his. Floyd held her and for a moment the only sound in the room was their harsh breathing. Their lips met. He watched her close her eyes, and then he closed his. Their kiss was a lingering, torrid one.

It broke after a minute or two. Heart pounding with anticipation, Floyd started to lead her toward the bed to undress her, and then stopped, frozen in mid-room, listening to sounds just outside the door.

"Something wrong?" Marie asked.

Floyd nodded. He put one finger over his lips to keep her quiet.

Then he sprang for the door and unlocked it and threw it open all in the same quick motion. His hands, the quick, deadly, powerful hands of a killer, shot out and clamped onto someone's shoulders, and yanked him into the room. Floyd slammed the door.

The man was an inch or two taller than Floyd, but lacked his compact hardness. Right now he was very pale, his light blue eyes flicking around nervously. He looked furtively at Marie and edged back away from Floyd.

"Who the devil are you?" Floyd asked.

"What do you care?"

"Maybe you're the house dick," Floyd said. "No, you would have identified yourself already if that's who you are. What were you doing outside my door?"

"Look, I was just passing by."

"I bet you were. Passing by, and you just happened to double up outside my keyhole."

There was no sense trying to get a straight answer out of him. Floyd moved swiftly and cracked the heel of his hand against the eavesdropper's cheekbone with jarring force, knocking his head back and stunning him. The man thrashed around, retching and gasping. Floyd spun in under the wildly waving hands and crashed two quick punches to the stomach. The intruder doubled up.

Floyd felt Marie's hands on his arms, trying to pull him back.

"Let him alone, Lee!" she said urgently.

He shook her off with an impatient shrug. Then he grabbed the eavesdropper by the neck and rocked him roughly back and forth.

"Who the dickens are you?" Floyd asked in a thick, menacing voice.

"I—I—" the man blurted, helpless, dazed.

"I know who he is," Marie said. "He's the tail that Howard pays to follow me around."

"You never told me there was one."

"I thought I shook him. I didn't want to get you nervous about him. He's a flub-dub anyway. The world's most amateur private detective."

"This true?" Floyd demanded, shaking him again. "You work for Gorman?"

The man nodded limply. "Don't hit me, huh? I was just doin' my job, that's all."

"He's always hovering around me," Marie explained. "Or trying to. But I found out about him early in the game. I can lose him easy as pie. Howard likes to make sure I go home to my own little bed like a good little girl every night. I thought I gave him the slip. His name's Eddie."

Floyd let go of him. Eddie stepped back, rubbing his throat at the collar. He looked scared out of his wits. With an imploring glance at Marie, he said, "I wasn't going to tell Gorman on you. Honest. I don't give a damn where you go or who you see. But I had to follow you, just to make it look official. Suppose he had a tail on me? I gotta watch these things."

Floyd eyed him. This was a complication he hadn't figured on. This bloodshot private eye knew that there was a connection between Marie and him. And then, when his client died tomorrow, and later, when Marie inherited, there could be trouble. But there was no way Floyd could take care of that now.

Floyd said in a very quiet voice, "Okay, Eddie. I'm going to let you get out of here. And if you say one word, half a word, even, to Gorman about where Marie went tonight or who she saw, I'll track you down, wherever you are, and I'll kill you, Eddie. I'll kill you."

The way Floyd said it, it left very little doubt of his sincerity. Eddie went even paler. Floyd stepped forward and hit him once again, a sharp backhanded rap across the face, just to make sure that Eddie got the message. Then he opened the door and pushed Eddie out.

"Beat it," he said.

Eddie beat it. Fast.

Floyd locked the door. His hands felt cold.

"Howard's always having me watched," Marie said. "That's one of the reasons why I hate him so much. He's such a mean, petty guy."

"You won't have to worry about Howard anymore after tomorrow night," Floyd told her. "But this character Eddie can foul everything up if he squawks."

"He won't."

"I wish we could be sure."

"Didn't you see how scared he was when you said you'd kill him?"

"I meant it," Floyd said. "But maybe he didn't realize that."

"He knew you meant it," said Marie. "The punk. Whatever Howard pays him, he isn't worth half of it. But let's forget about Eddie, huh?"

"Yeah. Let's forget about Eddie."

Marie leaned forward. Her heavy breasts, all but hanging out of her neckline, were an open invitation to grab her and bed her down.

Floyd didn't need any further hints. The time had come to cash in on that little promissory note Marie had given him that morning.

The time, in fact, was long overdue.

CHAPTER EIGHT

They kissed, and it was a wild, fiery kiss, and he grabbed Marie's breasts as though he had never held a girl's breasts before. Her body shimmied from side to side in voluptuous undulations.

Then he let go of her. He stared at her body, revealed by the tight clinging dress, and the hunger mounted in him until that was a raging fire. When it came to women, Lee Floyd had never been able to stay satisfied for long. Last night with Alice seemed like just something he had dreamed.

He wanted Marie. And he knew he was going to get Marie, Gorman's Marie, right now.

"Go on," he said. "Take your clothes off."

"Aren't you going to turn your back?" Marie asked in a sly voice.

"You want me to?"

"If you think you ought to," she said.

"Go on, take 'em off. I don't shock easy."

Marie laughed, then began to get out of her clothing.

She did a real production number. There wasn't any music playing in the room, but there might just as well have been some honky-tonk getting pounded out. Marie undressed like a girl who at least once in her life had been paid to strip in public.

Her hands snaked over her body. She found a zipper and pulled. She wriggled and shimmied and began to slide out of the gold lame dress.

She wasn't wearing a slip. There wasn't room under a tight outfit like that. Floyd watched, looking at the strapless bra that clung to her breasts, thrusting them upward and forward. Filmy black silk panties were stretched taut over her ample form. Her skin was very pale, very fair, the way a redhead's skin ought to be.

And her legs were magnificent. Stockings shaped their outline, and he stared at the white skin where the stockings ended. Marie smiled, obviously enjoying the glow of appreciation in his eyes.

Her hands went to the small of her back. She made a little gesture and the bra loosened. A shrug of the shoulders and the cups fell away.

Her breasts were bare.

They were big and firm, high and close-set, with a deep valley. Marie took a deep breath and her breasts rose outward in a way that made Floyd tingle all over. The nipples were very small, set in perfect circles of deep pink. Her nipples were rigid and excited.

Marie smiled. She brought one leg up, resting her foot on a chair. The flexed leg looked marvelous, absolutely perfect in contour and taper. Floyd eyed it as she undid the garters and slowly rolled her stocking down.

Then she switched to the other leg and took that stocking off too.

Then the panties. Inch by inch by inch, down and down. Off.

Nothing hid her flawlessness now except the garter-belt, tight around her waist, its straps dangling uselessly down. Marie didn't waste much time getting rid of it. She unsnapped it and flung it aside, and then she was completely nude before him. The sight of her hit him with as much impact as the sight of Alice's nakedness stepping out of the kitchen the night before.

He caught his breath, stunned by the wonder of her full breasts and slim body, and then he stepped back to get a better view. She stood there, smiling at him, her nude body radiating appeal.

"Let me see you," Floyd said. "All of you."

Marie nodded. She began to turn, slowly, like a mannequin on a revolving platform, letting him see the profile of her, the steep rises of her breasts and the sensuous curve of her buttocks and the flatness of her waist.

And then she had her back to him, and Floyd was able to see the smooth tapering curve of her shoulders down to the flat of her back, and the narrowness of her waist, and the sudden, astonishing flare at her hips, with heavy mounds of her buttocks.

"You look great," he said.

"Are you just going to look? You're allowed to handle the merchandise, too."

"Yeah," he said. "I was just getting around to that now."

Floyd reached out. One hand closed over the high peak of Marie's left breast. She swung around, turning toward him, and her mouth parted enticingly.

Her lips were soft against his. Roughly, he pressed her against him, splaying his hands out over the cool, silken-smooth bottom. While they kissed, she began to open his shirt.

Floyd relaxed his grip on her, letting her take his shirt off. Then her hand moved to his waist, and he laughed as she started his zipper for a moment and then yanked impatiently.

Suddenly she reached.

Floyd caught his breath sharply as her slim fingers found their target.

"You like that, huh?"

"You know I do," he said. "Go on, take all you want."

"There's plenty. A man doesn't have to be six feet ten to be the kind of man I like."

"Smart girl," he said.

She was breathing hard, her breasts heaving like big cannonballs. Her nipples were getting taller with each passing moment. She was opening his belt, now. In another moment he was naked in front of her, naked as she was. She took a good long look. Then she went to her knees.

Her lips were on him, her lips and her hands both. She was very coy, and very gentle. He looked at her, saw her head bobbing, and every moment sent a new pleasure over him. Excitement pounded in his brain. But this wasn't the way he wanted to take his pleasure from her, not at all.

He said hoarsely, "That's enough of that. Let's get down to the real business now, Marie."

She looked up at him, her face flushed, her eyes misty with desire. "Don't you like that, Lee?"

"Sure I do. But I like other things too, and I like them even better."

"What kind of other things?"

He nodded toward the bed. "Lie down and I'll show you, baby."

They went to the bed together. Floyd felt a sensation of delicious anticipation creeping over him. He had never expected this when he took on the Howard Gorman contract. It was strictly an extra, but the best kind of extra in the world. He wondered if Marie's performance in bed would measure up to the promise of her stunningly gorgeous body. There was no reason why it shouldn't, she thought. But you never could tell. You could never be sure what a dame was like in bed until you had actually had proof.

They snuggled up close. Floyd took her breasts to his kiss. One at a time. he kissed the high-peaked mounds of flesh. Marie moaned and whimpered with delight. She seemed to have terrifically sensitive breasts, Floyd noticed. Just touching them had turned her on. Kissing them like this seemed to send her into fits.

Then he moved lower. His busy lips explored and paid homage to her. Marie contracted her muscles in a reflex of pleasure while he caressed her.

And then he knew she was ready.

He moved back up the bed to her level. She lay on her back, her eyes slitted, her face flushed and sweaty with excitement. She smiled at him.

"Now," she said. "Take me, lover."

She seized him with her hands. Guided him.

He felt the wonderful warmth. There was always a thrill, the first time with a girl. You never know what secret, new magic she holds.

Her body quivered ... she undulated. At first slowly, then gradually she let the tempo pick up. Floyd began to shiver. He was keyed up to a fever pitch. Her kisses and caresses that morning had left him in a dither that had increased from hour to hour all day.

It would be so very easy to let go and take his ecstasy right now, in the first moments of their embrace.

No, he thought. Not yet. Not just yet.

Floyd wanted to show her that she had made the right choice, that she had picked a man for herself who could give her anything she could possibly ever want in bed.

He worked her for all he was worth.

He worked her till she was groggy with passion.

He took her up hill and down dale, through peak after peak. She moaned and gasped and sobbed and wept. Then she began to yell and shriek.

"Lee! Oh, Lee!" Her big breasts bobbled and jiggled as they thrashed around.

Her eyes fluttered open. She looked dazed with passion. Floyd was willing to bet she hadn't often been worked over quite this completely.

"Go on," she muttered hoarsely. "All the way, Lee!"

He grinned at her. Then he moved down the home stretch. She shuddered one last time, making a hoarse rattling sound of ultimate ecstasy. There was a quick burst of pleasure for him followed by others too fast to count, and they were finished.

That had been tremendous.

Poor old Howard, he thought. *I bet you never did that for her. And I bet you'd wish you could.*

Marie lay back, resting. The beads of sweat that had stippled her body were beginning to evaporate. Lee Floyd lay by her side, with his hand resting lightly on her middle. He was in a sort of half-doze; Marie wasn't entirely awake herself.

She felt the dull throb of the afterglow in her body. The lovemaking had been harsh and violent, had drained all the strength from her. He really believed in going all out, she thought. There had been a time, right at the supreme moment of the embrace, when she thought that all her nerves would short circuit if he kept things going much longer. But that had been the peak for him, too.

Marie let her hand rest gently on one of her breasts. It was about midnight, she figured. She had had a long, busy day. Dolores in the morning. Then dinner with Howard, getting him to change his will. Now bedtime frolics with a professional killer.

A busy day, but a fruitful one. She was an heiress, now. In line for a fortune. And the tough little man at her side was the one who was going to put that fortune in her hands, she thought.

Unless Eddie messed things up.

The stupid private detective had really chosen a devil of a time to get efficient. He had been following Marie around for weeks, now, always losing trail of her whenever she chose to dodge him. It became a kind of joke between them. She knew he was following her. She sometimes stopped to have conversations with him. But she had always shaken him off when going to visit Dolores. And she thought she had lost him tonight, on her way to the hotel.

She was wrong.

And so Eddie knew that there was a romance between her and a hard-faced little man with a room at the Ascot.

If Eddie went to Howard and reported that, everything would explode like a trainload of hydrogen bombs. She didn't think Eddie would, though. That was too risky.

But what would happen when Howard and Ethel Gorman suddenly died violently—the day after Howard had signed a codicil to his will naming Marie as his beneficiary? And then Eddie remembered that he had seen her with a tough, obviously criminal-looking stranger in the Hotel Ascot?

One of two things might happen. Eddie might go to the police, give them a description of Floyd, and suggest that they pick him up for questioning in the Gorman murder. Or else Eddie might approach Marie directly, and ask for hush money. That was a lot more likely, considering the sort of character Eddie was.

Maybe, she thought, the thing to do was have Eddie removed from the scene too.

But that would mean a third murder, and the more murders there were, the greater the chance that something would go wrong. Murder was too drastic.

There might be another way of keeping Eddie quiet.

I'll have a little talk with him tomorrow, maybe, Marie thought.

By her side, Floyd was beginning to stir.

"Come here, baby."

"I'm right here."

"Papa's in the mood again."

"So is Mama."

"What are we waiting for, then?"

They both chuckled. He put his hand to her breasts, and moved slowly along until it came to rest again. The powerful fingers began to move around skillfully.

There was nothing tender, nothing warmhearted about what he was doing, Marie thought. This was strictly business. He was handling her as though she were some kind of expensive machine that needed to be treated with care. She wasn't altogether sure she liked that style of loving. This was an improvement over Howard's clumsy flailing about, of course. But yet she was cold.

Cold as ice, she thought.

He kept his hand in place and leaned across her to kiss one of her breasts. Then he began stroking and working until he was cupping her buttocks.

"Yeah, baby," he murmured in the darkness. "That's the way. Let's take another ride."

She made him shiver as they started. And then she was having a direct hookup with the boiling intensity within him, with that cold purposeful energy that made him such a superb killer. His body acted in vigorous exertion.

But this time didn't last long. Not at all drawn-out like the first time. Inside of a few minutes, both of them were quivering on the edge of release. Her body rocked with delight as he clung to her. And then came the sunburst of passion, spreading over her entire body, every muscle was joyful.

For a long time afterward, they lay side by side again, body against body, both of them too tired to talk. Marie wondered what time it was. She looked for her watch and squinted at the tiny luminous dial.

Quarter to four.

"I better be going," she said.

"All right."

"You don't sound like you mind."

"I ought to get some sleep," he said. "I got lots of work to do tomorrow. It isn't easy work, either. Don't you think it is."

"How are you going to do it? With a gun?"

"The less you know about it, the better off you'll be, baby. Leave it to me."

"Don't let anything go wrong, Lee."

"If I do, it'll be the first time."

"Give me a kiss for luck."

"Yeah," he said.

His lips touched hers. His hands cupped her breasts briefly, then went to her buttocks. He let go of her. Marie rose from the bed.

She went into the bathroom to fix her face. She felt a little giddy, a little lightheaded. She splashed cold water in her face. She ran a cold washcloth over the globes of her breasts, and down over her belly. That was better. Home, now, for seven or eight hours of sleep.

She went back into the room. Floyd had turned the lamp on, and he was sitting up in bed with his arms behind his head. His body was lean and hard, without an ounce of surplus flesh on it.

Marie smiled at him. She looked around for her clothing. She found her panties and pulled them up over her lush buttocks and ample hips. She forced her breasts back into the confinement of the strapless bra.

Floyd didn't take his eyes off her while she dressed. Not for one moment.

She zipped up the dress, fluffed her hair back into place. She was ready.

"Okay," she said. "I'll see you."

"When?"

"Tomorrow afternoon, some time. I'll call you before I come over."

"Right," he said. "I'll be looking forward to that."

"It's only the beginning, Lee."

"Yeah," he said. "Well, I'll be seeing you, Marie."

She winked at him. Then she went out of the room. The moment she was out in the hall, she heard him locking the door behind her. He was a cautious one, all right. He never relaxed his guard, not even for an instant.

Poor Howard, Marie thought.

Poor Ethel.

Poor, poor Howard and Ethel.

And rich, rich Marie.

CHAPTER NINE

Floyd smiled to himself as he got back into bed. This had been a terrific night, a sizzling night, He thought about Marie and their two acts of passion, the long one and the short one. The hot one and the cool one. Quite a dish. He pictured her lithe nude shape next to him in the bed, thinking pleasantly of how nice this was going to be every night down there in Venezuela or Jamaica.

As soon as Howard Gorman was out of the picture, of course. And that would be pretty soon indeed. He pulled the covers up.

He slept.

At nine o'clock in the morning, there came the knocking on his door again. For the first bleary-eyed moment, Floyd thought that it might be Marie coming back again, but a second later he came to full wakefulness and knew that it was not Marie. It was the messenger service bringing him the rest of his cash.

But he didn't take it for granted.

"Who is it?" he asked.

"Acme Messenger Service, for Mr. Floyd."

"Okay."

He opened the door. It was the same messenger boy as the day before, carrying the same sort of thick manila envelope, carefully sealed. Floyd signed for it and took it. This time Floyd gave the kid a dollar. He was in good mood after having Marie.

The messenger brightened at the tip and said, "Thanks, mister! Say, you going to be getting any more of these things?"

"I'm afraid not," Floyd said. "But the buck ought to hold you for a while."

The kid went away. Floyd locked the door, broke

open the packet and the inner wrapper too. It was work to get it open, once again. But it was worth it.

The contents were the same as yesterday. Ten hundreds, twenty fifties, twenty-five twenties. Floyd stacked the bills up, putting the twenties on top. He looked down at Andrew Jackson's solemn, long-jawed countenance. Another twenty-five hundred crackers, he thought. Added to the package from yesterday, that made five thousand bucks he had received from Gorman. In cash. Without a whimper. All for killing old Ethel.

But what Gorman didn't know wouldn't hurt him for very long: that this day would see a second killing, one that Floyd would perform on the house.

With Gorman himself the victim.

Although he hadn't had much sleep, Floyd didn't feel like going back to bed just now. He decided to get up and have breakfast, and take a nap again around noon. That would leave him rested up for tonight.

The phone rang.

He grabbed at it. "Hello?"

"Floyd?"

It was Gorman. "That's my name," Floyd said

"The package ...?"

"I got it," Floyd said. "Just now. Everything's okay. You want a receipt or something?"

"I just wanted to know if we were on schedule."

"Sure, Mr. G. Tonight's the night."

"When?"

"Midnight, just like I said."

"I'm counting on you, Floyd."

"It'll go smooth as clockwork," the killer said. "Just relax and leave it all to me."

Gorman rang off. Floyd put down the phone. Gorman had sounded okay. Not suspicious at all.

Apparently Eddie had kept quiet about last night. The threat had worked, and the detective hadn't reported the incident. If Gorman ever found out that Marie had come here and seen him—

Floyd scowled. He wished there was some chance of disposing of this Eddie. He had dangerous information inside his skull, and, considering the overall situation, the smartest thing to do was to give Eddie's skull a little ventilation. If the private detective reported to Gorman that Marie and Floyd had seen each other in Floyd's hotel room, there was bound to be a mess.

Well, nothing he could do about it now. There was a joker in the deck, though and Floyd wasn't happy about that. He took a quick shower, shaved, dressed, went down to breakfast.

There was still plenty of preliminary work to do. By way of establishing an alibi.

Marie woke.

It was noon, Saturday. The big day, the day that murder would be committed. She was in such a relaxed and cheerful mood that it surprised her. Considering how much was at stake today, she had figured she'd be edgy. Instead she was blithe as a bird.

The will had been changed. Howard was going to die. She was going to be rich.

She had a lot to do today, too. She had to see Eddie and get things straightened around with him. After that, she'd go over to visit Dolores, probably, since that was how she usually spent her afternoons. Finally, she'd drop in on Lee Floyd and give him some encouragement for the big night. Then she'd sit back and wait for the headlines to be made.

Nude, Marie walked into the bathroom of her

luxurious little apartment and took a good shower. Then she fixed breakfast for herself. She got dressed while the eggs were cooking. Pedal-pushers and blouse comprised her Saturday costume. Nothing fancy. Not after spending most of yesterday wearing various strapless bras that pushed her poor breasts every which way in the name of beauty.

A little after one o'clock Marie went downstairs, into a bright, shiny, sunny day. Where was the detective, now? He worked Saturdays, Marie knew. He went on duty around noon, and tailed her all during the day. A heck of a way to earn your living, she thought. Especially when you were as lousy at it as he was.

She looked around. There he was.

He was sitting in a parked car across the street.

Marie waved to him. He pretended to be ignoring her. She started to go across to him, and he got out of the car and tried to slip away.

"Eddie!" she called. "Hey, Eddie!"

He turned and gave her a sour look. He shook his head as though telling her that this was no way for her to behave toward her shadow.

"Wait a second," she said. "I want to talk to you, Eddie. Will you wait?"

The private eye shrugged. He slipped his hands in his pockets and stood there dejectedly as Marie came up to him. She flashed a brilliant smile.

"How are you?" she asked.

"Lousy. If you really want to know."

"Poor Eddie. He gave you a rough time last night, didn't he?"

"He sure did."

It showed, she thought. His face was bruised and puffy-looking. He still looked pale and jittery.

Marie said, "You were pretty dumb. Skulking

around outside the hotel room. What were you trying to do, grab a cheap thrill? If you weren't going to report it to Howard anyway, what was the point of coming upstairs?"

"Just keeping tabs," Eddie said. "I got to earn my money somehow. But it's all over. I'm quitting. Today's the last day I follow you around."

"I'll miss you, Eddie."

"I bet you will. But I got to quit this job. Last night was too much. You fool around with dangerous guys, and I'm not out to get roughed up."

"You think he's dangerous?"

Eddie shrugged. "I don't know who he is, but the way he looked at me, I thought I'd have a stroke. I don't want to run into that guy again, and I don't want to cross him or anything. So I'm quitting. I'm finishing out the week."

"Does Mr. Gorman know this?"

"Not yet. I'll tell him on Monday when I hand in my report."

You won't be telling Howard anything on Monday, Marie thought. Because Howard isn't going to be in any shape to listen to you.

Marie said, "Listen, when you hand in that report, Eddie—"

"Yeah?"

"You aren't going to say anything about where I went last night, are you?"

He looked unhappy. "I told you, I wasn't going to say a thing about that. You think I want trouble from that guy you went to? What do I have to gain by telling Gorman about it? I'm quitting him anyway."

"There's a smart boy," Marie said. "You stick to that way of looking at things and you'll go far."

"You can count on me. I'll keep quiet."

"Okay," Marie said. "But I want to make sure

you go on keeping quiet about it after you quit Gorman."

"I don't get you."

She said, "This guy I was with last night, he's pretty tough. I think you know that. As a matter of fact, he's got a record as long as your arm. I wouldn't want anyone to ever know that I had anything to do with him. You know. It wouldn't do me any good to have a reputation for consorting with criminals."

"Yeah," he said. "But who would I tell?"

"I wouldn't know about that. But just in case anybody, any time in the future, asks you was I seen in the company of a guy fitting that description, you say no. You don't know a thing. Okay?"

A clumsy look of shrewdness came into the private detective's eyes. He said, "You trying to cover up for him on something? You afraid of getting mixed up in something he's done?"

"I just don't want any complications," Marie said. "I want you to keep shut. And I'll make it worth your while to forget about yesterday."

"Worth my while? How?"

"How would you like to go to bed with me, Eddie?"

His eyes widened. His cheeks turned red. "Well ..."

"Interested?"

"Sure I am. When?"

"How about right now?"

"I'm supposed to be keeping an eye on you."

Marie laughed. "Here's a chance to keep a lot more than an eye on me Eddie. Let's go upstairs. I'll show my appreciation for your silence."

"Well, gosh," he said. "Sure thing!"

Marie was smirking as she turned away from him. The poor goofball was practically frothing at the mouth. He was starry-eyed with desire.

She wasn't exactly overwhelmed with the yearning to go to bed with him. But this was a cheap enough price to pay for buying his silence. He would come to realize, eventually, that he had compromised himself pretty thoroughly by climbing into the hay with the woman he was supposed to be trailing. And so, when his client died tonight under suspicious circumstances, and his client's girlfriend was already known to be consorting with a mysterious tough guy, the detective would have a good and substantial reason for keeping his mouth shut and not taking his obvious conclusions to the police.

They went upstairs and into her apartment. The detective looked around in awe at the place. Marie shrugged. It wasn't as fancy as all *that*, she thought.

"Want a drink first?" she asked.

"Not really. Not unless you do."

"I can skip it."

"So can I."

He gave her an idiot grin. His fingers were twitching a little. He looked so eager to have sex that he was downright pathetic.

The private detective wasn't really a bad-looking guy, Marie thought. He was young, sort of thirtyish, a little above medium height, something on the beefy side. What he was missing wasn't anything physical. There was an attitude that he didn't have. When Lee Floyd looked you in the eye, he was telling you with every inch of his body that he was hard and tough and didn't take no for an answer. When this guy stared at you, it was in a soft and foolish way that didn't exactly set your heart on fire. Devil only knew what had persuaded him to become a detective, Marie thought.

"Get undressed," she said.

"Sure," he simpered.

They began to peel off their clothing. Marie got her blouse off fast, then the pedal-pushers. She stepped out of her undies. The detective stripped away his clothing.

Naked, ready for business, he didn't look quite so boring. Marie felt the tips of her breasts beginning to tingle as she stood nude before him. Almost any man could do this for her. She was lucky that way.

"Come on," she said huskily.

Eddie grinned. Then he came toward her. He came very close, his gaze eager. He touched her breasts, lightly grazing them with his palms. He was breathing hard, practically snorting. Then his hands moved farther, over the firm flesh of her bare buttocks, and then over her legs.

"Lie down, "he said.

"Yeah."

They settled onto the bed. His hands moved everywhere over her body. His lips found hers. He was still a little hesitant, as if perhaps he didn't really believe that this was actually happening.

Marie's hand moved down his body and let him know that this was real.

He gasped. Then suddenly he made his move.

He wasn't a very skillful lover, or a very tender one. There was a certain raw energy about him, and that was all. Marie didn't care. She wasn't marrying him, after all. She was just bribing him.

Her body worked in triple time. Get this over fast, she thought. The faster the better. He won't mind.

She put on a good show. She moaned and panted and hissed. She raked at his back and shoulders with her nails, drawing red furrows in the sweaty flesh. Leave some souvenirs on him, she thought. A few nice scratches to remember her by.

"Oh—oh, yes, baby, yes!" she cried.

He moved faster. So did she.

Marie sensed a spasming, but that wasn't really much, because Eddie wasn't much of a lover. She magnified that, to give him the impression that he had really sent her rocketing to orbit somewhere. Her entire body shook and shivered. She dug her fingers deep into his back.

He gave a long hoarse moan of ecstasy.

Then that was all over. He lay still for a while, his beefy body like a corpse. He was crushing her breasts. But she didn't want to rush him. Let him think he was really something, she figured.

Eventually he got up. He looked dazed and happy. His eyes were shining as he stared at her nude form.

Marie lay still sprawled on the bed, giving the detective a good look.

"Gosh," he said. "Gosh, I'm going to remember that for a long time."

She fluttered her eyelashes at him. "So am I, Eddie, so am I."

"And you can count on me. Mum's the word."

"I appreciate that, Eddie."

He stared lovingly at her bare ruby-tipped breasts, at the white magnificence of her skin. A big school kid, she thought. A real goof. Leave it to Howard to hire somebody like that. He could have been a lot worse, after all. A whole lot worse.

"You'd better go now," she said.

"Yeah. Sure."

He began to look around for his clothing. Marie helped him collect his things. She bustled around, nude and enticing, now and then grazing his arm or back with the bare globes of her breasts. She was seeing to it that he'd leave here so lust-dazzled that he couldn't possibly ever turn her in to the police, not even for double parking.

She kissed him good-bye, pressing herself languorously up against him. She kissed him with lips and tongue, with everything. When she let go of him, he was bright red in the face, and blinking his eyes at her in bewilderment and pleased shock.

"So long, Eddie."

"Yeah, Marie."

"I'll remember you."

"You think I won't?" He grinned happily. "This was a big day for me, Marie."

"Me too, Eddie."

She blew him a kiss as he opened the door. He took one last look at the lush nudity of her, his eyes traveling sappily over her breasts and legs, and then he was gone.

Idiot, she thought.

Cretin.

Well, she wouldn't have to worry about him anymore. And the price had been pretty cheap. Fifteen minutes of sweaty lust for a lifetime of luxury, she didn't mind paying that at all.

The moment the door closed, Marie headed into the bathroom. A good quick shower and she felt decent again. She came out, towelled herself briskly, and went to the telephone. It was early afternoon, now, almost two o'clock. She figured Dolores would be up by this time.

She dialed her friend's number.

The phone rang five times. Frowning, Marie wondered if Dolores had gone out. Then someone picked up at the other end.

"Hello?"

"You want some company?" Marie asked.

"Oh, hi, Marie. You mean right now?"

"That's when I mean," Marie said.

"Sure. Come on over."

"I'm on my way," Marie said.

CHAPTER TEN

Lee Floyd was busy that afternoon. He had an alibi to establish. He didn't think he would need it, but he believed in covering his traces wherever he went. Just in case he had to explain where he had spent this evening, he intended to have a cover story.

He went downstairs and stopped off at a travel agent's booth in the lobby of the hotel. A cute, busty clerk with short strawberry-blonde hair smiled at him in a say-hello-to-the-customer way, then picked up some of his magnetic sex appeal and took a deep breath to push her breasts forward in a rather more familiar fashion.

"Can I help you?" she asked throatily.

You sure can, baby, Floyd thought. Out loud he said, "I'd like some information."

"Certainly."

"I'd like to take somebody very important to a Broadway show tonight. But I haven't been keeping up with the reviews. What's the best show in town right now?"

"Musical or drama?"

"Musical, I guess."

She thought for a moment. Then she said, "*High on the Totem Pole*, that's the biggest hit this season."

"Fine," Floyd said. "I guess I'll get tickets to that one, then."

"For tonight?"

"Yes."

"You'll have a hard time," the girl said, smiling. "It's supposed to be sold out until Christmas."

"You mean I can't get tickets at all?"

"I didn't exactly say that. It's hard to get tickets. If I were you, I'd try one of the ticket agencies. Don't waste your time at the box office at all."

"Is there any agency you'd recommend?"

"The Empire's a good one," she said.

"Where's that?"

"Broadway, around 47th or 48th. They're likely to have tickets for almost anything. Of course, it'll cost you, you know."

"That's okay. I'm prepared to pay."

He thanked her and walked out into the street. Her little sigh of excitement didn't go unnoticed. She was item one of his alibi—the travel agency girl who wasn't likely to forget the exciting-looking man who had asked her how to get tickets for *High on the Totem Pole*.

But he needed more links in the chain.

He took a cab across town to Broadway and made his way through the Saturday afternoon crowd of strollers into the street-floor office of the ticket agency. A dapper-looking man came to wait on him.

"I'd like two orchestra seats for *High on the Totem Pole* for tonight," Floyd said casually.

The clerk smiled condescendingly "Surely, sir, you know what a big hit that is."

"Of course. That's why I want to see it."

"It's sold out until the end of the year."

"At the box office," Floyd said. "But I understand you people can get tickets for almost anything. I'm entertaining someone very important tonight, and I want nothing but the best for her. I'm willing to pay, if I have to, but I want those tickets."

The clerk was silent a moment, obviously sizing Floyd up. Floyd knew about the New York City law governing ticket-scalping. The agencies that dealt in theater tickets were prohibited from charging a premium greater than about a buck and a half per ticket over the box office price. But a show like *High on the Totem Pole* was a "hot ticket," and seats for a

Saturday night could bring a fat price in an under-the-counter deal.

After a moment the clerk said, "Will you excuse me? I'll see if we can serve you."

He disappeared into a back room. No doubt they were loaded with tickets—for sale only to the right people at the right price. Most likely they were conferring in there as to whether Floyd qualified as "right people." For all they knew, he was a city inspector coming around to find out if they were scalping seats.

The clerk came back. He looked stiff and uneasy. He said, "As it happens, sir, we do have a pair of tickets for tonight."

"Swell!"

"But we try to reserve such tickets for visitors to New York. You must understand that we try to give preference to out-of-towners, whose opportunities to see our shows are limited."

"That's fine," Floyd said. "I'm from Ohio, and I'm in town just for a few days."

He took out his wallet and showed the clerk his Ohio driver's license, just flicking it in front of the man's nose long enough for him to see what the document was. Floyd also incidentally happened to let the man see the thick wad of greenbacks bulging in his billfold.

The clerk's demeanor changed instantly. He smiled and said, "In that case, sir, we'll be glad to supply you with the tickets. Except—" He lowered his voice. "You have to realize that in the case of a show like this, the normal prices don't apply."

"Of course."

"It's a little irregular, but we have to do it. If we sold the tickets at the legal price, we'd take a considerable loss ourselves."

"Certainly."

"And so ..."

"How much are they?"

"Twenty dollars apiece," he said.

"Sure," Floyd said. "That's about right, I'd say. It's only fair."

He plunked four ten-dollar bills down on the counter. It was a pity to throw away so much money, but it simply had to be chalked off to the overhead of the job. He didn't care to work without an alibi. And, getting five thousand bucks to do the job, he couldn't begrudge wasting forty.

Besides, there was all that extra money that Marie would bring along when they teamed up later on.

The bills disappeared from the counter in nothing flat. The clerk handed Floyd two green tickets in a little white envelope. Nine-sixty apiece for the seats, and ten-forty apiece for graft. A nice racket, he thought. But the profit comes in little chunks.

He said, "I was thinking about going to a night club after the show. Could you give me some advice?"

"Certainly."

"Do you think I'd enjoy the show at the Latin Quarter?" Floyd asked.

"It's a very good show."

"Swell," Floyd said. "We'll go there. I guess I'll need a reservation, eh?"

"It's a wise idea."

"What time will the play be over?"

"Quarter past eleven," the clerk said.

"Then I'd better make my reservations for twenty after eleven. It must fill up fast after the Broadway shows let out."

The clerk nodded. He pointed to a pay telephone in the corner of the agency. "If you wish, you could call them from here."

"I think I will," Floyd said.

He thanked the clerk and went into the booth. He made a reservation for two, in his own name, at the Latin Quarter for 11:20.

Everything was set, now. The theater tickets gave him an alibi through 11:15. After that, the Latin Quarter would serve. And so, at midnight, when Howard and Ethel Gorman met their deaths, there would be plenty of proof that he had been dozens of miles away, living it up in New York City.

Marie rang the bell of Dolores' apartment and waited. A few seconds went by. There was no response from within. She was just about to ring again when she heard sounds from the other side of the door, and then it opened.

Dolores grinned at her.

"Hi," she said. "Come on in."

Dolores was nude except for a pair of black silk panties. The heavy, hard-tipped globes of her breasts rose and fell enticingly. She turned, leading Marie into the apartment without kissing her hello. Casually, she peeled away her panties and tossed them toward a chair. Marie stared at her friend's pink nude buttocks.

Dolores said, "Hal! Hal, come on out!"

Marie frowned. "What ...?"

"A friend," Dolores explained. "You don't mind, do you, darling?"

Marie stood there gaping in astonishment as a man emerged from the bedroom. All he wore was a pair of striped shorts. He was strikingly handsome, a big, rangy man of about thirty-five, well over six feet tall, with a powerful physique and a lean, hard body. His arms and legs were extraordinarily long, his shoulders were athletically wide, his hips were slim. His muscles were the flat kind rather than the bulging kind, but he looked incredibly strong even without the weight-lifter style of development. A thick, coarse mat of dark hair covered his chest.

He smiled amiably at Marie.

Dolores said, "Marie, this is Hal Barker. I met him last night. He's a real great guy. Hal, I want you to meet my best friend, Marie Caldwell."

"How do you do," Hal said, in a deep, rich bass voice.

Marie didn't know what to make of any of this. She had come over here expecting to get some friendly Lesbian loving, and instead it turned out that there was a man present. Dolores hadn't said anything about having company when Marie had phoned her a little while before.

Marie said, "If I'm interrupting anything—"

"Don't be silly," Dolores said.

"I don't want to be an intruder."

"You aren't, honey. Hal asked me to invite you over. He wanted to know if I had any friends."

"I was in the mood for a little three-way fun," Hal explained gently.

Suddenly Marie understood. "You mean you and Dolores—Dolores and me ..."

"One big happy family," Dolores said.

Hal grinned. "You look like you'd enjoy a deal like that, Marie. Why don't you get all those silly clothes off yourself and make yourself comfortable."

Marie nodded vaguely. It was a curious situation. Right now, Dolores was completely nude, Marie was completely dressed, and Hal was clothed only in the strategic place. Marie's nipples throbbed with need. Making love to Eddie a little while ago hadn't exactly satisfied her, though she had pretended to the

detective that he had. She had come over to Dolores'
place expecting to finish what Eddie had begun.

But that didn't necessarily have to be finished in
the Lesbian way.

A glance at Hal told her that it was ten to one he
was terrific in bed. He had grace and agility and
strength, and plenty of poise and self confidence
besides. Marie had never known a man who had all
those traits who wasn't a superb lover.

But, of course, Dolores was here. So it would be
all three of them in a scramble on the bed. All right,
she thought. She glanced at Dolores' nakedness,
eyeing her friend's firm white buttocks with mounting
eagerness.

Hal was busy pouring drinks. He came across the
room and put one in Marie's hands.

"Here," he said. "I think this'll do you some
good, Marie."

She nodded and took the drink from him. Dolores
casually sat down and crossed her legs. She leaned
back, her breasts rising and falling gently.

Marie tasted the drink. It was strange, an
unfamiliar taste but a pleasing one.

"What am I drinking?" she asked.

"A Pisco Sour," Hal said. "Pisco's a Peruvian
brandy. I brought a bottle for Dolores."

"Hal's an airline pilot," Dolores said. "He goes
back and forth between here and South America all
the time. He's going to Brazil in a few days."

Marie took another sip of the drink. She said,
"Where'd you two meet?"

"He picked me up right in the street," Dolores
said. "He's got an eye for available women."

"I was tired of airline stewardesses," Hal said.
"The pickings are too easy there."

Marie laughed. The more she listened to this man

and looked at him, the more interested in him she got. She took a deep sip of her drink. Then she put it down and said, "I might as well get as comfortable as you two are."

With mounting inner excitement, Marie began to undress. She pulled her blouse off. Hal's eyes centered on her. Marie smiled at him. She felt a little self-conscious, undressing in front of the two of them. She had been in plenty of odd situations in her time, but never anything that was quite like this.

She unzipped the pedal-pushers and pulled them down over the ripeness of her hips. Underneath, all she was wearing was a pair of gauzy yellow panties that didn't hide much.

Marie saw the muscles bunch along Hal Barker's lean jaw. He was interested. Obviously. Even though he had probably spent a wild night with Dolores, he was still able to get excited by Marie as she undressed.

Quite a man, she thought.

She reached for her bra hooks.

A snap and a twist and the straps dropped away. The cups fell from her breasts, and with a gay flip Marie sent the bra sailing away to join her blouse and her pedal-pushers. She filled her lungs with air, and her breasts swelled outward, twin mounds of fleshly delight.

Hal's eyes gleamed with eagerness. He smiled in approval of what he saw. Marie heard Dolores give a little gasp of Lesbian excitement. They both desired her, Marie thought pleasantly. And they both were going to get her.

She rolled the panties down and stepped out of them.

Now she was nude.

"There," she said. "We're so much more

comfortable this way, right?"

"Much," Hal said.

"But now you're the one who's dressed," Marie said. "Come on. It isn't fair for you to be covered up while we're both naked."

"She's right," Dolores said.

"Glad to oblige," the pilot replied.

He jerked at the snap of his shorts. The garment dropped to his ankles, and he kicked it off. Marie caught her breath as she looked at him. He was magnificently male, one of the most virile specimens she had ever seen. Her excitement must have been apparent, because Hal grinned at her as though pleased by the change of expression on her face. Marie's heart pounded.

He glanced toward the bedroom.

"Shall we?" he said.

"Why not?" Marie replied.

She gulped down the last of her drink. He turned, went into the other room. Marie followed him, with Dolores bringing up the rear.

The bed was rumpled and disheveled. Marie knew that Dolores and Hal must have had a wild, wild bout last night. While she had been at the Ascot with Lee Floyd, Dolores had been giving herself to Hal. And now was going to be Marie's turn with the long-legged pilot. Her throat went dry in anticipation of pleasure.

They stood by the bed. Then Hal came forward and Marie glided to him and pressed herself tight.

She kissed him. Passionately.

He held her tight. She could sense the virility of him, the strength of him.

The next thing she knew, she and he were on the bed and Dolores was there too, and the three of them were in a wild tangle and Marie was aware that Hal was cupping her breasts and taking them to his lips to kiss, and that Dolores' breasts were pressing close as she kissed and caressed her.

Marie gasped and sighed. This was too much, to be loved by both of them at once. She thought she was going to go out of her mind from sheer excitement. Hal's lips on her breasts, against the nipples, and Dolores' lips moving here and there, unpredictably.

Then Hal withdrew.

"Go on," he said. "Now just the two of you. I'll watch the first round."

That wasn't the way Marie would have preferred. She had known Dolores many times, and Hal never at all, and she wanted to be loved by the big man. But he had called the tune. So she would have to wait a little while longer to give herself to him.

Hal rose from the bed. He took a ringside seat on a chair in the corner. Dolores squirmed and thrust herself against Marie. Marie felt a surge of excitement. The presence of a highly attractive man in the room as a witness to their illicit affair only added a special spice to the mixture, she thought.

Marie reached out. Her hands found the ripe mounds of Dolores' breasts. Dolores' nipples were like cherries sprouting in fleshy abundance. Marie gripped Dolores' breasts, passion taking a breathtaking hold of her, and put her lips to Dolores'. Their mouths met. Dolores' lips were sweet and exciting. Marie felt Dolores' hands stealing over her body, stroking her. Marie put one hand around Dolores to the flawless globes of her buttocks.

Body sighed against warm body as ecstasy possessed them both.

They were old hands at this game by this time. In the months since they had become Lesbian lovers, the two girls had made love often, and they knew one another intimately, knew what gave pleasure and what did not, how to touch off a flurry of delighted sighs and gasps, how to move onward along the road of pleasure.

They loved each other with their fingertips and their eyelashes, with their lips and breaths, with the grazing tips of their breasts. All their skills as Lesbian lovers came into play now.

Hal was getting something to remember, Marie thought. He was witnessing quite a performance.

Marie's body entwined itself. Her lips met those of Dolores; her flesh touched ecstatically against that of the dark-haired girl. Then their bodies pivoted, as they had done so often before, and they gave each other mutual pleasure that sent them rocketing along the path to bliss.

And then they were in each other's arms again, and passion took hold of them. They soared higher and higher, into the loftiest realms of ecstasy, and passion came in a searing burst, and they sank back together, panting, gasping, exhausted.

Then Marie became aware that someone was joining them in the bed.

Hal.

Strong masculine fingers closed at the ripe, lush hillocks that were Marie's breasts. His breathing was hoarse, fiery with lust.

He embraced her fiercely.

"My turn," he said.

CHAPTER ELEVEN

Howard Gorman nervously paced from room to room of his elegant Long Island mansion. The afternoon was trickling away, crawling second by second. An eternity was going by in one afternoon.

It was three o'clock, now. Nine more hours to midnight, Gorman thought.

Nine hours, and then Lee Floyd would make him a widower.

Right now it seemed to Gorman that midnight would never come. Midnight was a billion years away. He could do nothing but pace. There was a dryness in his throat, a hard knot of tension in his belly. He walked from room to room of the lavish $150,000 house.

He passed through the panelled library, with its rows of leather-bound books. Through the conservatory, green with Ethel's collection of strange plants, cacti and other exotic growths. Through the living room with its heavy-framed oil paintings. The dining room. The kitchen. Restlessly, he prowled the house.

Ethel was outside, pottering in the garden. He went to a dining room window and looked out at her, saw the stout, gray-haired woman bending low to pull weeds from the rock garden near the patio.

Nine hours is all you have left to live, Ethel, Gorman thought.

He felt no regret about it, only impatience that it would not happen for so many more hours. Looking at the chunky woman in the garden, Gorman found it hard to believe that once she had been slim-waisted, lovely and young. That vast bosom of hers had once been girlishly full. But Ethel had changed with the years, and now the time had come to get rid of her and take someone young and passionate.

Marie.

Gorman began to tremble at the mere thought of her. To hold her in his arms, to have those breasts against his body, to run his hands down her satiny back to the wondrous globes of her buttocks—

Yes!

Yes, that was worth killing for!

Gorman smiled. Cold beads of sweat went trickling down his skin. He began to pace again. He wandered back into the library, stared idly at the rows of books that he had never read, the handsome leather-clad editions that the interior decorator had purchased because they gave such a wonderfully nineteenth century look to the library. The sets of Dickens and Thackeray and Waiter Scott, Gibbon and Parkman and Prescott. Volumes of poetry by the dozen. Shelley, Keats, Byron. Tennyson. Kipling.

"Do you like Kipling?" he would ask Marie.

"Yes," she would answer. "I love it. Let's kipple right away."

He bit his lip. Soon, soon, Marie would be his, all the time. They would lie on a tropic beach, under a blazing sun, and they would swim in crystal-clear waters, and then they would sit on a terrace in crisp evening clothes, having dinner and sipping rare wines, and the tawny tanned torso of her would rise out of her low-cut white dress, her breasts a temptation that no man could resist, and they would dance after dinner and, then they would go to their room, and undress, and their bodies would join for hours of mad, voluptuous passion.

He put Kipling back on the shelf. He looked at his watch. Ten past three.

Eight hours and fifty minutes left, now.

He wandered into another room. Ethel was

coming in from the garden, now. Gorman knotted his hands together, cracked his knuckles.

Ethel said, "The pachysandra is all overgrown with weeds, Howard. I absolutely must speak to that gardener about it. He hasn't done a thing there in months."

"By all means, Ethel," Gorman said. "Speak to him. Tell him all about it."

"First thing on Monday," she said.

"By all means."

He nodded and began to walk away from her. Ethel said, "Are you feeling all right, Howard?"

"I'm fine. Why?"

"I don't know. You seem so restless. So much on edge today."

"Just a passing mood."

"You keep roaming from room to room."

"I'm getting exercise."

"Why didn't you play golf today?"

"I wasn't in the mood," he said. "Maybe I'll go tomorrow. Yes. A good idea."

"You could use the fresh air," Ethel said. "You look so peaked these days. As though you've been worrying about something, Howard."

"I've been very tied up in a big project," he said. "But it'll be taken care of soon. Very soon."

Marie shivered in delight as Hal Barker's hairy, muscular body embraced her. He seemed to radiate virility.

He said, "That was wonderful, watching you two. But I don't think I could have held out for very much longer."

Dolores rolled to one side. Marie moved to him willingly, savoring the rugged strength of him. He kissed her, a hard, savage kiss. There was stubble on his face after his overnight session with Dolores, and the bristles jabbed against her skin almost painfully. His hands gripped her breasts.

And, as he enthusiastically explored the hills and valleys of her body, Marie gasped and quivered in renewed expectation of ecstasy.

Dolores remained nearby. There wasn't an atom of jealousy about her, and she seemed pleased to have turned Hal over to Marie. She clung to Hal, crushing her breasts against his back even as he caressed Marie. Marie sighed and panted. Although she had just experienced the summit of bliss in the arms of Dolores, she was always greedy for more, always ready for a second, a third, a fourth round.

Especially with someone as exciting as Hal.

He seemed just as eager to have her as she was to be had. He covered her with kisses and caresses while she panted in delight. As Hal touched her, Marie reached out and encountered the taut globes of Dolores' breasts and grasped them, so that all three persons on the bed were intertwined in a complex tangle of flesh.

Marie yearned for the beginning.

"Take me," she whispered.

Hal smiled at her. His body went taut, and he clasped her to him. Marie bit into the firm flesh of his shoulder, and closed her eyes and readied herself, and he took her.

This was heavenly. He was thrilling her while Dolores hovered nearby, also caressing her. This was a fantastic situation and a fantastic group of sensations. Hal loved her with smooth grace, with a virility that Marie had never experienced before, not even with Lee Floyd. He was almost a superman, this handsome, long-limbed man. Right in the first moments of their lovemaking, Marie sensed that he could do things to a woman that most men only dreamed of being able to do.

Dolores was nearby in all her female abundance, and Marie felt pleasure coursing toward her from two sources at once. Her entire body trembled. Every nerve, strung tight as a bow-string, twanged with pleasure.

Marie gasped in a delirium of lust as Hal stirred her emotions to the peak of no return. He was so very masculine that there was some pain in the embrace, but there was ecstasy, too. He gripped her tightly, his hands digging into the yielding flesh of her firm buttocks. He worked again and again. She eddied higher, toward the spiraling dizziness of absolute ecstasy, and her whole being responded to the double excitement.

Marie closed her eyes and his hands were at her breasts and Marie reached out and found the fullness of Dolores' lovely bosom.

And then the explosion of lust came.

That was an incredible, wonderful moment, as she lay there, finding pleasure with both of them simultaneously. A dazzling, pinwheeling skyrocket of sensation struck her, nearly lifting the back of Marie's head off. Every muscle and nerve in her body twanged. She clung to Hal, gripping him desperately, nails digging into skin, her face showing the eager urgency of her emotions.

The thunderous tide of passion rolled over her and knocked her for a loop.

The sensations were so intense that she began to black out. A wave of torrid, dizzying impulses rocked through her brain. She stayed conscious, but the world seemed to spin around her, and she fell back, warm and dazed and fulfilled, her brain reeling.

She was hazily aware that Hal had taken her to

the ultimate moment without reaching his own completion. That was amazing, that he could have given her such sublime pleasure without going all the way himself. He was so virile a lover that he was evidently able to exhaust one woman completely and turn instantly to the next.

Dolores was ready. Ready and in a hurry.

"Hal!" she panted. "Hurry! Hurry!"

Hal took her.

This was a stunning thing to see. Marie stared in astonishment. She had never before been this close to another couple loving.

As Hal and Dolores abandoned themselves to their lust, they began to make harsh, bestial sounds of delight. Marie watched their sweat-shiny bodies. Hal drove with unquenchable energy. He pushed Dolores swiftly to a peak of passion, made her gasp and pant. She slipped back, went on to another and another. And Hal tirelessly guided her from one crest of passion to the next again and again.

Didn't this man ever get tired, Marie wondered? Didn't he ever want to finish?

Dolores was almost in a state of collapse now. She made an odd choking sound, sucking air deep into her lungs. Hal took that as some sort of signal to redouble his efforts. He worked with desperate fury.

They were near the finish, now.

Dolores was moving frantically. Hal's face was thrust against the pillow, and his body, with sweat streaming from him, was moving like some machine running wild.

Marie, watching in stunned fascination, saw the sudden rigidity of Dolores' body as the impact of ecstasy hit her.

And then that ended.

Marie put her hands to Hal and held him. She

could share his pleasure with Dolores. His hoarse gasps told the story of his superhuman exertions.

That was over. Exhausted, Hal and Dolores lay back.

Marie stared at them. She felt an ache of new lust in her own body. Even though her bout with Hal and the one with Dolores had left her satisfied, watching this furious session had excited her again.

Dolores' eyes fluttered open. She said, "That was pretty good, wasn't that?"

"Some show," Marie agreed.

Hal grinned at them both. "Let me tell you, you're quite a team, girls." He reached out and cupped two pairs of breasts in a friendly way. Then he lay back. "Who's going to get me a drink?"

"I will," Dolores said.

She padded across the room and into the other room, where the ingredients had been left. Marie settled back, nestling in Hal's arms after watching Dolores' bare buttocks vanish from the room.

"Glad you came over?" Hal asked.

"You bet I am."

"I thought Dolores was pretty wild," he said, "But I didn't expect her to have an even wilder friend."

She smiled. He cupped her breasts cozily.

He said, "What are you doing tonight?"

"I'm meeting a friend for dinner."

"And afterward?"

Marie shrugged. "I'm free after eight, nine o'clock. You want another three-way get-together?"

"No," he said. "Just two ways."

"Cutting Dolores out?"

He nodded. "She's a good kid, and I don't mean to do her wrong. But I've got some things I'd like to discuss with you. Plans. And she just doesn't fit in with them, I'm afraid. Do we have a date?"

Marie looked at him strangely. Tonight was the night that Lee Floyd would be carrying out his double act of murder. At midnight, out in Long Island. She'd need something to do to while away the tense time.

"All right," she whispered. "It's a date."

Dolores came back into the room, carrying a tray of drinks. The bare hills of her breasts jutted out pleasantly over the tops of the glasses as she carried the tray at waist level. She smiled at the couple in the bed.

"Don't that look cozy," she said.

"We're just waiting for you, baby," Hal said.

"Let's take a breather first and have some refreshments," said Dolores.

She handed the drinks round—Pisco Sours, again. Marie gulped half of hers down quickly. It was amazing what a thirst all that exercise could give you, she thought.

It was still early in the afternoon, too. She was supposed to call Lee Floyd at five or six o'clock, and spend dinnertime with him, give him a sendoff for the business he had to perform tonight. But that still gave her a couple of hours for amusement here.

Hal's exertions seemed to have told on him. He appeared to be quite definitely out of commission, at least for the time being. He sat back quietly, sipping his drink. Marie and Dolores sat alongside him on the bed, and he playfully caressed them both, now running a hand down Dolores' smooth, tapering legs, now reaching out to cup one of Marie's firm taut breasts.

After a while Hal said, "I feel almost ready to start again. Almost, but not quite. How about the two of you trying again while I watch. That ought to warm me up again."

Marie looked at Dolores. "You game?"

The sudden stiffening of Dolores' rosy nipples gave the answer away in advance.

"You bet," she said.

Hal pulled himself up, leaving the bed to have a clear view of the action. Marie moved toward Dolores and embraced her. She pressed her face against the steep hills of the dark-haired girl's breasts, played with them, kissed them excitingly.

Soon they were both panting and gasping once again. It was easy to get excited this way. Marie had the feeling that she could love thirty, fifty, a hundred times today. She could take on a whole regiment, and then a platoon of WACs besides. She was mile-high, thinking about the cascade of money that Lee Floyd's two murders were going to dump into her clutches tonight.

She and Dolores climbed the path of pleasure together. Higher and higher, faster and faster,

The peak was in sight, now. Eagerly, frantically, they embraced. Ecstasy swept over them both.

It was a pounding blaze of lust, consuming Marie. When the tide of passion receded, she felt weak and tired, and longed only to pillow her head against Dolores' bosom and drift away into sleep.

There wasn't going to be any repose for her right now, though.

Dolores slid backward, making a little sighing sound of satisfaction, and an instant later Hal was in bed with them again. He took Marie by the wrist, pulled her away from the groggy, slumped-over Dolores. His eyes were blazing with lust. He looked as though he hadn't seen a woman in months. He had completely revived, simply by watching the two girls in their Lesbian embrace.

"I want you," he said hoarsely.

"Take me, then."

He fell to her. She gave herself quickly and easily, her body lust-happy now, caught by a mad whirl of passion that seemed to have no end. They swept upward together, reaching the summit at about the same time. The volcanic eruption of their need hit them in a single instant. The world seemed to blur for Marie. Quivering delight overtook her for what seemed like the millionth time that endless afternoon.

The orgy ended. This time Hal was through. So was Dolores. She was sound asleep, her long-limbed body sprawled out in delightful nude abandonment, black hair veiling her lovely face. Hal looked drowsy.

"Go to sleep too," Marie whispered. "Rest up for tonight, Hal."

"Not a bad idea. You?"

"No," she said. "I've got to go."

He reached for her and ran his hands lightly over the firm melons of her breasts. "I'll see you tonight, though."

"Yes," she said.

"Where shall we meet?"

"My place is the best."

"Where's that?"

She gave him the address. He repeated it and nodded. "I'll get there around nine, all right?"

"Fine." she said. She would see to it that he stayed past midnight, maybe all night. That would be best. If any question arose about her whereabouts on the day of the murder, she could bring him forth to testify that he was in bed with her at the moment that Howard and Ethel Gorman were being killed. It would be a fun kind of alibi to establish, too.

Hal settled down, nestling his head against the firm soft mounds of Dolores' breasts. Marie smiled. Nude, she tiptoed into the bathroom and began to clean herself. She got under the shower for what seemed like the fiftieth time today, though actually it was only the third. Her body felt a little tender from all that lovemaking. Even after she had washed herself thoroughly, she felt a slight discomfort.

Hmm. And now she had to go over to Lee Floyd. And he would surely want to love her too. For luck, before the murder. First that sap Eddie, then Dolores, then Hal, then Dolores again, then Hal again—and now Floyd—

A busy day. Too busy.

The thought of having to submit to Lee Floyd's roughhouse style of lovemaking right now didn't appeal to her very much. She needed a rest. Delicate tissues were starting to swell from overuse. And if she was going to spend the night with Hal Barker, she would certainly be in for another energetic workout then.

She couldn't skip seeing Floyd.

Well, there were ways of loving, and then there were other ways of loving. She would try one.

She dried herself off and went back into the other room. Hal and Dolores were sound asleep. Like babes in the woods, Marie thought. She began to dress.

Neither Hal nor Dolores woke up. Marie went over to the bed and kissed them each lightly, putting her lips against Dolores' breasts, then kissing the man at an even more exciting place.

Marie beamed.

She had to thank good old Dolores for this delightful afternoon. She was very, very grateful indeed.

She was walking on Cloud Nine as she went out of the apartment. Lee Floyd awaited her.

CHAPTER TWELVE

Lee Floyd got back to his hotel room a little before five that evening. Everything was set up, and now he just had to be patient until it was time to go out to Long Island and pull the job.

He felt pretty calm. Why not? It wasn't the first job he had handled. He wasn't expecting any particular difficulties. And the rewards were big, this time. His fee, his five thousand bucks, that seemed like a pitiful sum next to the real payoff.

Marie.

And Howard Gorman's money.

He grinned at his reflection in the mirror, and sat down at the desk. He took out the pack of cards and began to lay out a hand for Poker Solitaire. He began to play, choosing his cards slowly, knowing that every moment that ticked away brought him closer to the time of the murder.

He would be glad to have the job behind him. But then would come the hard part: sitting around New York City for a couple of days, waiting. It was a natural temptation to try to clear out as soon as possible after committing a murder, but that was just the sort of thing that was asking for trouble. In case he happened to be under police surveillance—though he doubted it—they would certainly nab him if he made a sudden break from the city right after a crime. Whereas if he hung around, doing the tourist bit, it would throw them off suspicion.

He picked up his cards, put them in place. The phone rang.

"Hello?" Floyd said tightly.

"Baby, this is Marie."

"How are you?"

"I'm great," she said. "Never felt finer. What

about you?"

"A-okay," he said.

"Listen, Lee, I met Eddie—you know, the detective Howard hired. I talked to him."

"Yeah?" Floyd tensed. "What did that dodo have to say, anyway?"

Marie laughed. "He's still scared purple from last night. You really made an impression on him. He told me that he's quitting his job with Howard on Monday. He thinks that it's too dangerous."

Chuckling, Floyd said, "He'll be unemployed before Monday, whether he knows it or not. But you say he sounded scared, huh?"

"Very much so."

"Think he'll keep quiet?"

"I know so. I had a long talk with him. He's got no guts, Lee. He isn't going to file a report on our meeting. He won't say a word."

"Good."

"I know you were worried about him knowing, so I thought I'd tell you you didn't need to be worried anymore."

"Thanks," Floyd said. "When am I going to see you?"

"How about right now?"

"Why not?"

"I'll be right over," she said.

"Okay. Look, I've got theater tickets for half past eight. Tickets for two, but there's only one of me. You want to come along? The show's a good one. It's *High on the Totem Pole*."

"I've seen it."

"Come along anyway," Floyd said. "I don't want to walk in alone."

"All right," she said. "I'll go in with you. But I can't stay. I—I'm meeting a girl friend at nine o'clock,

Lee. I think I ought to be with somebody tonight, and it can't be you."

"Smart," he said. "Okay. You come on over here. We'll have some fun and then we'll have some dinner and then we'll go over to the theater. You can leave any time you like, as long as you're seen going in with me."

"Good enough. I'll be right over."

"I'll be waiting."

She didn't take long. Floyd had time to put the cards away and comb his hair, and then came her light rap-rap on his door. Cautious as ever, he did a double-check before he let her in.

She was wearing a blouse and tight slacks, and she was a glorious sight to see. Except that she looked a little weary around the edges.

"What's the matter?" he asked.

"What do you mean, what's the matter?"

"You look peaked. Kind of pale."

"Do I?"

"I guess you're not getting enough sleep," he said, smiling.

"Maybe I'm not getting enough love," Marie countered, chuckling a little.

"I doubt that."

"How would you know?"

"At least I'm doing my best," he said. "Come on, I'll give you another dose. How's that, Marie?"

"Sounds great."

She glided into his arms and he kissed her. His hands roamed her body, exploring all the soft, lush contours of her, contours that he had come to know very well in the last thirty-six hours. The more he was with her, the more he wanted her.

When they broke the clinch, they were both

breathing hard. They began to get undressed.

She said, "You feeling relaxed?"

"About what?"

"Listen to him! About what! About tonight, of course, dodo!"

"Sure I'm relaxed," Floyd said evenly. "Is there any reason why I shouldn't be relaxed?"

"I don't know. Some people might feel a little edgy—about—you know."

"Not me," he said. "It's my business. My profession. Why should I feel nervous? I know what I have to do and I know how I'm going to do it."

"Yeah," Marie said. "But don't you sometimes wonder if something's going to slip up?"

"It never has."

"There's always a first time."

"You're a cheerful one, aren't you? You out to jinx me or something?"

"Don't be crazy, Lee. I was just wondering. You seemed so cool. I wondered if it was just a pose, just an outside façade."

"It's real," he said.

"I wish I knew how you could be so cool about something like that."

"It takes practice, baby. But let's not waste time talking about it. We have more important things to do right this minute."

She threw a sizzling smile at him. "Yeah," she said, rolling her panties, her last garment, down over her hips and off. "Important."

He came toward her.

He reached out and touched her, his hands gliding into place over her bare breasts, and it was like flipping a switch. All Marie's seeming fatigue and weariness dropped from her, and she came to life in a startling way. The moment Floyd's hands found those heavy globes of ripe, luscious flesh, Marie began to pant and gasp. Marie seemed to be on fire now. She was moaning and jiggling and jumping, wild and eager. She tugged him over to the bed and they stood next to it, arms about one another.

She was so nearly his height that this was a convenient arrangement, legs against legs, lips to lips. Her mouth worked over his mouth and moved around.

Her eyes were slits of desire. Her face looked distorted and puffy with excitement.

Then she broke away from him and stepped back a few paces to look at him.

"Tell me something," she said.

"Yeah?"

"You know about the French way?"

Floyd shrugged. "What French way?" he asked. "That could mean almost anything."

"I mean this," Marie said, turning and wiggling at him in a provocative way. "Like that. You want to?"

"I never thought much about that."

"I'm in the mood for that."

"Bored with the regular way?" he asked.

"Variety's the spice of life, don't you think? C'mon, be a sport."

Floyd was puzzled by her eagerness. He had never felt much yearning to love that way, but he didn't have any particular objections. And if Marie was so anxious for that all of a sudden, well, it wasn't any difficulty for him to oblige her.

"Okay," he said.

"Swell."

She moved toward the bed. Instead of lying down, Marie took a different posture. She crouched, kneeling at one side of the bed with her body bent. Her back was to him, enticingly displayed.

"So?" she said. "Where are you?"

"On my way," Floyd said.

Floyd slipped his arms around her, moving them down the satiny front of her body, covering the full globes of her breasts, squeezing them, sending her into new raptures of desire. Her nipples were against the palms of his hands, like little smooth pebbles.

He slipped one hand down her front and her middle. Then he moved close behind her to the soft cushions of her buttocks.

He met resistance.

"I'll hurt you," Floyd said.

"You don't need to worry about that," Marie said urgently. "Just start."

Sure thing, he thought. Whatever you want, girlie. Just say the word.

He moved with sudden vigor and took her like she wanted him.

Marie gasped. It was a sound unlike any sound Floyd had ever heard any woman make before, a deep gasp that wrenched out of the uttermost depths of her. It was a low, hoarse, grunting sound that seemed to rise from her toes and gather strength as it swept to her lips.

Then she quivered convulsively and began to move, pressing fiercely.

Floyd moved his arms around to the front of her again. He found the ripe cones of her breasts and splayed his hands out over them, holding them tight, with the nipples trapped by two fingers of each hand.

He was still afraid that he might be hurting her. But obviously he wasn't. She seemed to love that. Not only that, she wanted more than he was giving her. She reached around and clamping her hands on the small of his back, and urged him even harder.

"Go!" she urged. "Go! Go!"

"Yeah, baby!"

She was leaning far forward, now. And she began to move. Slowly, at first, in a wide circle, and then more wildly, a rapid dance that sent pleasurable sensations over Floyd. A type of sensation he had never experienced before.

This was quite a chick, he realized for the millionth time. She had plenty of special talents. She could really thrill a man, in fifty or a hundred different ways. He figured that he was never going to be bored with her, when they were living down in Latin America spending Howard Gorman's hard-earned dough.

Her hips were really dancing around, now. As the intensity grew, Floyd tightened his grip at her breasts, closed his eyes, bit down hard on his lips, tried to hold himself back.

Marie was moaning now, wailing wildly in banshee howls of pleasure. This strange way of love evidently was something she dug to the core. Her whole being was trembling in passion.

All of a sudden she froze.

All motion ceased.

Marie half rose, and clamped thrillingly, her muscles acting. Then she let out a long, loud sigh that he recognized as the beginning of ecstasy.

"Now!" she cried. "More, Lee!"

He smiled. He let himself go. Her body quivered and shook. She was running wild now. And at the height of her frenzy, he took his own pleasure from her, again and again and the two of them went skyrocketing off to the promised land in a blaze of glory.

Then they rested. And after a while she got up and yawned and stretched voluptuously.

"What time is it?" she asked.

"Almost six."

"I ought to get going."

"Where to?"

"Back to my place to change," she said. "I can't go into a restaurant with you in pedal-pushers. Or to the theater, for that matter."

"Yeah," he said. "Okay. We'll meet for dinner, then. There isn't time for you to keep going back and forth. Where do you want to eat?"

"Someplace nice."

"You know this city a lot better than I do," Floyd said. "You pick it."

"How about a steak house?"

"Why not?"

"Okay, then. We'll eat at Marty Ryan's. You know where that is?"

"Not really."

"Sixth Avenue and 53rd. You better phone for reservations. I'll meet you there at quarter to seven, okay?"

"Good enough," Floyd said.

He put his arms around her. The heavy globes of her breasts rolled from side to side against his chest. His hands slid down and cupped her buttocks. Then he released her, and she began rapidly to dress. He waited until she was ready to go.

"Marty Ryan's, quarter to seven," he said. "See you there, kid."

She blew a kiss at him. Then she was gone. Floyd let out his breath in a hiss of relaxed delight. What a broad that one was! She was worth giving up a lifetime of one-night stands for. All she was was the best-looking chick he had ever known, and the wildest besides. And she was the sole heiress to hundreds of thousands of dollars. What more could a guy ask for, anyway?

He phoned the restaurant, made the reservations. Then he took a quick shower and got dressed.

This was it, he thought.

Before he came back to this room, he'd have added two murders to his string.

Now that the waiting was over, now that the evening of the killing had finally come, Floyd felt totally nerveless. He hadn't had much sleep all week, what with the bus ride from Cleveland one night, and Alice the next, and Marie the night after that, and those early-morning messenger deliveries getting him out of bed. But his eyes were clear and his hands steady despite his lack of sleep and his fierce physical exertions of the past few days.

Killer nerves, that was what they said he had. And they were right.

Sure. When the time came to squeeze the trigger, Floyd knew that he would need only one bullet apiece. He did nice, neat jobs.

Before he got into his clothing, he oiled his gun again. He made sure it was in good shape. The gun was a fine precision instrument, he thought, sleek, graceful, cool to the touch ...

... like Marie, he thought. *Just as deadly ...*

She danced through his brain. He couldn't stop thinking about her, thinking of Marie's eyes, Marie's breasts, Marie's lush, curving buttocks. She was sort of a dream girl, hard and yet soft, cold and passionate, all at the same time. In his calm, icy way, Floyd analyzed the situation and had to admit to himself that he'd fallen perhaps a little too hard for his own good. Getting involved with a woman—even a woman like Marie—made him vulnerable in a way he wasn't used to.

But he couldn't help that now. He was hooked on her, but solid.

And by nightfall Howard Gorman would be dead, and Marie would be his alone.

Everything was set. He had his alibi more or less established. He had the round-trip tickets to Hewlett, Long Island, the town where Gorman lived. Floyd had bought them at Penn Station this afternoon, since it might attract too much attention if he were seen buying them late at night. Someone in the ticket booth might remember his face. The one part of the operation that was most delicate of all was getting on board the train to Long Island, because his alibi wouldn't be worth a plugged nickel if he happened to be spotted as the only man buying a ticket to Hewlett on the late train.

About half past six, he was ready to go. He holstered the gun deep within his jacket and locked up the room after one quick look around.

In the lobby, he stopped off at the desk and told the desk clerk he was going out for the evening, in case anybody called. Casually, he added that he had tickets for *High on the Totem Pole.*

The clerk congratulated him. "It's not easy to get tickets to that, sir!"

"I know," Floyd said. "I really had to work at it, let me tell you."

"It's supposed to be a great show."

"That's what I hear. I hope so. I'll be making this a real night on the town," Floyd said. "After the show I'll go on over to the Latin Quarter for a while. Most likely I won't get back here till two or three in the morning."

The clerk beamed. Floyd hoped that all the details had registered. Every little link that he added to the chain of his alibi helped.

He hailed a cab outside the hotel, and ten minutes later he was at the steakhouse on 53rd Street. Marie wasn't there yet. Floyd told the head waiter about the reservation and the man nodded and said, "Would you care to wait at the bar, or should I show you to your table?"

"At the bar, I think."

"Very good, sir."

Floyd settled down at the bar next to an animated, breasty blonde who was making time with some man she had obviously picked up a little earlier that day. Amused, Floyd listened to their conversation for a couple of minutes. Then the bartender glanced at him.

"What's yours?"

"Ginger ale," Floyd said.

"*Just* ginger ale?"

"Just ginger ale," he repeated crisply.

He got a peculiar look, but he let it pass without reacting. On this night of all nights, he needed his reflexes to be at their best. No liquor, of course. Not even beer or wine, tonight. Ginger ale would do.

He drank it quickly. Then Marie came in.

"Marie!"

"Hello, Lee."

She came to him. She looked radiantly beautiful in a tight, low-cut dress. The white globes of her breasts were thrust upward and outward in stunning display. Everyone in the restaurant swivelled around to look at her—the men for the obvious reasons, and the women to see what all the fuss was about. Floyd felt a surge of warm pride. They were all staring at his woman.

Soon to be his, anyway.

He gave her his arm. The head waiter showed them to their table. Her eyes were glowing with excitement. This was going to be a big night, Floyd thought. The biggest night in his life.

CHAPTER THIRTEEN

Marie wasn't really very hungry. It had been a long, exciting day, full of surprises, and she didn't think that the butterflies in her stomach were likely to appreciate having chunks of steak dumped on them. But, appetite or no, it was the polite thing to do, to eat, when Lee Floyd was offering hospitality.

She wasn't able to pack the food away the way he did, though. She did all right with her appetizer, the shrimp cocktail, while Floyd gobbled up a tray of cherry stone clams. But she began having trouble with her onion soup halfway to the bottom of the bowl, and Floyd had to finish it for her after he had polished off his own.

The main dish posed some troubles, too. The cold mashed potatoes went down fine, but it was hard work eating the rare sirloin. Marie was a little surprised at that, because usually she could eat all the steak anybody cared to put in front of her. Not tonight, though.

Too much was on the line tonight.

Howard Gorman was being murdered tonight.

Floyd grinned across the table at her as he hacked away at his steak.

"Having trouble?"

"A little."

"What's the matter with your appetite?"

"I guess I don't have much tonight," she said.

"Maybe it's the steak. We can send it back if you don't like it."

"It's a terrific steak. It's my fault."

"Go on," he said. "Eat. There's nothing to be nervous about."

Marie shook her head in admiration. "I don't understand how you can just sit there belting the food away as though—"

"As though what?"

"As though this was any ordinary Saturday night."

He grinned at her. "It is," he said.

He popped another slab of steak into his mouth. Marie sighed and cut a small slice for herself. She'd be glad when this night was over, she thought. Suppose he bungled the murders? Suppose Howard didn't die? Suppose ...

No, she thought. Floyd was a pro. Everything was going to come out all right.

And afterward she'd have Howard's money. And all the time in the world for spending it.

When they were getting down to dessert, Floyd began looking repeatedly at his wristwatch. It was the first sign of nervous tension he had shown all evening.

"Afraid we'll be late for the show?" Marie asked.

"It's after eight o'clock."

"Curtain's at eight-forty, isn't it? We've got lots of time."

"Not so much. I think we'll skip coffee, if it's okay with you."

Marie managed an edgy smile. "What's the matter? You in such a sweat to see the beginning of the show?"

"I don't want to get there late," he explained in a low voice. "I want to be in my seat when the curtain goes up. Latecomers get stared at. Someone might see me and remember my face."

"I thought that's what you wanted," Marie said. "Isn't that the whole point of going to the show tonight—to be seen and noticed by people?"

"Not by people in the audience. If they notice me coming in, they may also notice that I leave early.

And that might touch off some suspicions in their minds later on. It's safest not to let the opportunity arise."

"Sometimes you can be too cautious."

"It always pays off," he said. "Let's get out of here, shall we?"

He called for the check. Marie watched him pay it with a crisp twenty-dollar bill. Part of the money Howard had given him, she thought. They left their seats.

All eyes followed her as they went out of the restaurant. Marie smiled. She enjoyed having people stare at her that way. She knew she had a good body, and she liked to show off.

Floyd got a cab. As they rode down Broadway to the theater, Marie said, "You know, I won't be staying at the show more than about fifteen minutes."

"That's okay. Just so long as you go in with me. That's all I want."

"What if I'm seen leaving?"

"It won't matter. Just try not to kick anybody in the shins on the way out."

They got to the theater about ten minutes before curtain time. A crowd of well-dressed people milled about on the street outside. Floyd cut his way through them, elbowing a path. Marie followed along.

She watched him closely. When he gave his tickets to the man at the door and got the stubs back, he smiled and said, "Thank you very much."

The ticket taker looked puzzled. People weren't in the habit of saying thank you to him as they surged past into the theater.

"He'll remember me, I think," Floyd said.

Inside, he halted in front of the table where a boy with slicked-down hair was selling souvenir programs.

"Get your program booklets!" he was calling. "Only a dollar! Souvenir program booklets!"

"I'll take two," Floyd said.

The boy smiled. "That'll be two dollars, sir."

Floyd pulled out his wallet, thumbed through the bills, frowned, and finally handed the boy a twenty-dollar bill.

"I'm sorry," he said. "It's the smallest I seem to have."

The program seller looked irritated. He put down his thick stack of glossy programs to get the change together, and carefully counted it out: a ten, a five, and three singles. Floyd took the bills from him and let them drop. They went fluttering to the lobby floor, and there was a momentary confusion as people picked them up and handed them back to him. Floyd thanked everyone profusely.

Then he turned to the program seller again and said, "Can you tell me what time the show starts?"

"Twenty to nine, mister."

"And when it ends?"

"Quarter past eleven," he said, staring bleakly at Floyd and not bothering to hide his feelings of annoyance at this clumsy geek with the big bills and stupid questions.

"Thank you," Floyd said. "Thank you so very much."

He turned to Marie, and they moved on through the lobby into the theater.

"He'll remember me, I think," Floyd said.

"You have a regular technique for this, don't you?"

"I want to be noticed coming into the theater. I want the employees to see me, not the other members of the audience. They're no good, because they can't be traced in case I need to subpoena them."

"Have you ever needed to use any of the things you've planted?"

"Never," Floyd said. "But it pays to be careful."

They entered the orchestra section. A faded blonde usherette with washed-out blue eyes showed them to their seats, and Floyd managed to compliment her gushingly on the color of her lipstick. She looked at him blankly, in complete and utter astonishment.

That was another one who'd remember him, Marie thought.

They took their seats. Floyd said, "When you leave, go out the side way. Use that door over there. I think it leads right to the street."

"Okay."

"You won't meet any of the people we've just seen, if you go out that way."

"I understand," Marie said.

"And afterward don't call me tomorrow at all. I don't want to hear from you until Monday afternoon. Tuesday would be even better. No matter how big a temptation it is, don't call me."

"You think it's dangerous?"

"I don't know," he said. "Let's play it safe, huh? We can always gab later on."

She nodded. Her heart began to pound tensely. He was seemingly so cool, thinking of everything, rattling off precaution right and left. Would he slip up somewhere? Would he overlook anything?

The house lights began to dim.

The curtain rose and the overture began to blare.

Floyd settled back in his seat. Marie sat bolt upright, edgy, fretful. She thought about Hal Barker. The airline pilot was supposed to meet her at her apartment around nine o'clock. She had made that date before she realized she would be serving as part of Floyd's alibi. Now, she couldn't get to her apartment herself much before quarter past nine, she knew.

Would Barker be prompt?

If he'd only be fifteen or twenty minutes late, there'd be no problems. But he was a pilot, after all, accustomed to living by timetables. Most likely he'd be there on the dot of nine. How long would he wait before he decided that she had stood him up?

It would be terrible if he rang the bell, found nobody home, and went away. Marie wanted desperately to see him again. Tonight, when she was so tense and fearful on account of the murder scheme, she wanted a man in her arms, holding her close until dawn. And Hal Barker was a terrific lover. She had found that out a few hours before. Tonight was her chance to have him all to herself, without Dolores cutting in for her share.

The show hadn't been going for more than five minutes when Marie said, "I've got to leave now."

"All right," Floyd whispered. "Talk to you Tuesday, Marie."

She gripped his hand for a moment. "Good luck."

"Yeah," he said.

She slipped from her seat. Luckily, it was right on the aisle, so she could get out without having to disturb too many people. She circled swiftly around the theater, and pushed open the door marked EXIT. It led her into an alleyway, and the alleyway took her out to West 45th Street.

It was a few minutes before nine o'clock. The traffic jam of the theater hour had all but ended, now. Every one of the many theaters along Broadway had its show underway now, and the congestion of forty-five minutes ago no longer existed.

"Taxi!" Marie called.

A cab pulled up. She ran to it, her breasts bobbing against the scoop front of her dress. A moment later, she was on her way east.

It took time, though, even with the streets relatively traffic-free. Red lights halted them at Sixth Avenue and again at Fifth. It was quarter past nine before the cab pulled up in front of the apartment house where Marie lived. She tossed some money at the cabbie and sprang out.

She rushed into the house. The elevator was waiting in the lobby for her. Marie got in, jabbed at the button, and the car took off.

It reached her floor in nothing flat. Marie got out, turned to her left, started to walk down the corridor toward her apartment.

Hal was leaning against her door, waiting for her. He stood there with arms folded and a quizzical smile on his face. One eyebrow lifted in mock annoyance as Marie approached.

"You're late," he said.

"I'm terribly sorry, Hal. I was delayed. Anyway, I didn't think you'd really show up on the dot."

"Men in my line of work usually respect a timetable," he said. "Anyway, I was impatient. I got here at quarter to nine."

"You've waited half an hour for me! I was afraid you'd leave if you didn't find me here."

"I can be very patient when beautiful girls are concerned. But I doubt that I would have stayed here waiting for you much past midnight. How about inviting me in, now that you're here."

Marie smiled and unlocked the door. They went in. He didn't waste any time surveying the apartment. The moment the door was closed, he reached for her and pulled her into his arms. Her body crushed up against his. He kissed her hungrily, passionately. It had been only five or six hours ago that he had been wallowing around in bed with two beautiful girls. Yet his kiss was so torrid it might have been five or six years since he had last seen a woman.

He let go of her. Marie took a deep breath. "Those kisses are bad for my blood pressure," she said.

"They're swell for mine, though."

"How about something to drink?"

"Love it."

"I can't offer you any Pisco, though."

He shrugged. "I'll settle for plain old bourbon, if you've got some. The fancy things can get tiresome after a while."

"Do you feel the same way about women?" Marie asked slyly.

He looked straight at her. "No," he said. "There are some women you can't get tired of at all, no matter how hard you try. But there aren't many like that."

She kicked off her shoes and got the bourbon out, humming a little wordless melody to herself. Hal settled down on the couch, crossing his long legs. She brought him his drink.

"I'm going to get into something comfortable," she told him. "I won't be but a second."

She went into the bedroom and began to get out of her clothes. Nude, her breasts swaying and bobbing, Marie went to her dresser to find something to put on. There was nothing more comfortable than nothing at all, she thought. But it didn't seem really proper to entertain company in the nude. There was time for peeling down to the buff later on in the evening.

She found a shortie nightgown that would do. It was black and just about transparent, and came down to her hips and no further. A pair of matching panties protected her maidenly modesty, more or less. Marie grinned at herself in the mirror. The nightgown revealed the heavy globes of her breasts, the rosy rises of her nipples, her buttocks. But she didn't think that Hal Barker would object much to the view.

She went back into the living room and posed enticingly for him.

"How's this?" she asked.

"Great," he said. "Just great."

She settled down on the couch with him after she had fixed a drink for herself. His hand slid around her body, and cupped itself over the ripe sphere of her left breast. She waited for him to pull her madly against him and start to make love, but he didn't.

"Let's talk business," he said.

She looked at him in surprise. "Business?"

"That's right."

"What kind of business?"

"You-and-me business," he said. "I told you, I had a proposition to discuss with you. And I want to discuss it before we get distracted by other things."

"Okay," Marie said. She tucked her legs underneath her body and looked up at him in open curiosity. "Go ahead, then. Discuss away."

"I talked to Dolores about you. She says that you keep company with some middle-aged man, but that you aren't particularly fond of him. Right?"

"Right," Marie said. "But—"

"Let me finish. In fact, let me start. The pitch is this, Marie. I'm going to be transferred to a strictly South American run. I'll be flying mostly from Rio de Janeiro to Lima, Peru. Back and forth across the continent. Sometimes down to Buenos Aires, and sometimes over to Caracas, but mostly it'll be the Rio-Lima run. I have an apartment in Rio already.

It's a pretty swell one, I have to admit. Right on the beach, in one of those big white apartment houses. Have you ever been to Rio, Marie?"

"No."

"It's quite a place," Hal said. "The climate's perfect, the people are great. From my apartment you can step right out and go swimming. You can't imagine a lovelier setup. There's only one thing missing from the picture."

"What?"

"You." He grinned at her. "The senoritas are fine but I happen to like American girls better. What I'm looking for is an intelligent, attractive, sophisticated chick who wants to set up housekeeping with me in Rio. To share my apartment, rent free and all expenses paid. I'm up here shopping for a roommate right now. Think you're interested, Marie?"

"This is kind of sudden."

"I know it is. But that's how I do things. I'll arrange for you to fly down to Rio free, whenever you can close out your affairs here. Next week, the week after—take a month, if you have to. Or come down on a trial basis. Any way you like. I saw enough of you this afternoon to know that I want you, Marie."

Her eyes sparkled. Excitement was stiffening her nipples.

"Tell me more," she said.

"There's not much more to tell. I'll be away from the apartment three days out of every week. I'm a liberal sort, and you can spend those three days any way you like, so long as he's out of the apartment by the time I get back."

"That's pretty fair."

"And as I think you discovered today, I also go in for combination deals. So do you, it appears. We can set up all we want of those down there. I won't mind a bit. I've got some cute little Brazilian chicks in mind that I think will really turn you on."

Marie's head whirled with excitement. To live in a beach-front apartment in Rio, to share her nights with Hal and Hal's girlfriends, to experience all the gaiety of Latin America at its best.

But she already had a commitment to go away with Lee Floyd.

The choice was before her. The dashing, romantic airline pilot or the hard, enigmatic little murderer? One offered her gaiety, excitement The other was putting a fortune into her pocket, but what were the risks of living with him, Marie wondered?

She weighed the options.

Hal said, "Well? What do you think of the idea?"

"It's pretty grand-sounding."

"Does that mean yes?"

"Give me some time to think about it, Hal."

"How much time is some time? A week? A month? Eleven years?"

Marie laughed thinly. "Say, five or six hours," she told him. "Enough time for me to get to know you a little better."

"You already know me pretty well, I'd say."

"In bed," she said. "Now let's get to know each other the other ways too."

"Does that mean we don't make love this evening?"

"We'll have time for that too," she said.

"Come here."

"If you insist."

"I insist."

She slid across the couch to him. His hands roamed her, began to draw her nightgown off. She helped him. Then he got to his feet. Unhurriedly, he began to strip off his own clothing. Marie watched him.

His body was bare, now. Long and lean and rugged and masculine. Naked, he came toward her. Marie smiled in eager anticipation. Her eyes traveled down the length of his body, down the muscular surface of him, and halted in the middle of the journey. He was ready for love. Marie reached out, her hand lovingly caressing him.

She dropped to her knees beside him.

She gave him pleasure carefully. She knew just how far to go. She knew when the point of no return had been reached with a man, and she took care not to reach it with him. Just when he was wild with excitement, Marie rose, her eyes gleaming brightly.

Both of them were ready, now.

He caught hold of her and they went sprawling together to the living room floor.

The deep pile carpet caressed Marie's bare back and buttocks. Hal lay by her side, his hand roaming her body, but she felt no need for preliminaries now, not on this day of passion when every conversation seemed to end in love.

"Take me," she gasped. "Don't wait, Hal! Take me!"

He smiled with cool self-possession, moved toward her and she accepted the weight of him.

He started easily.

A little hiss of air escaped Marie's lips and her lips sought his, and for a while neither of them moved, as they lay there simply glorying in the fact that they had achieved the most exciting thrill that was possible for two human beings.

Then they started.

He was a skilled lover in the highest degree. He took the lobe of her left ear with his teeth, and playfully nibbled it, and Marie responded with passion. He swung his head around to cover her right breast, and he kissed the nipple, and Marie responded with little shivers, with muscular spasms that foretold the great eddying sensations that would be rocking her in a little while.

Sensation was flooding over her from a dozen places at once. She gave herself up fully, enjoying the way he took command of her. He was completely in charge. Marie gasped and shook. She moved rhythmically, and for each motion of hers there was a matching motion of his, and she shivered at his perfect rhythm, and knew that he would last as long as she needed him to last. Sweat ran off her body. Her eyes were tightly shut.

Her hips were moving. She felt his hands underneath her. He was ever so gentle. Marie helped, rising away from the floor, offering herself to him.

"I'm almost there," she gasped.

"I know."

"This is the most wonderful feeling, Hal."

"Yes. Yes."

"Hold me. Dig your fingers in."

He dug his fingers in. She could feel him grasping as a sudden ecstasy swept her body.

Again.

Again.

"Hal—"

She couldn't get out another word. She threw her head back and opened her mouth, filling her lungs with air as the gasping hit her, and the fury swept through her again and again, and he moved, and she moved, and they moved, and this went on happening, on and on as he effortlessly lifted her from peak to peak.

Higher.

Higher.

And still he carried her higher as the waves of sensation slammed again and again, each time a little stronger and a little sweeter, until her whole being quivered with delight and she shook with the towering explosion of flaming desire that smashed over her like fire as she arched again and again, straining to rip every ecstasy from the awesome power of Hal Barker's raging virility.

And still he waited, the strength of his control surging through him like the ripple of tough muscle as he led her up the peaks of fulfillment.

Still higher.

Higher yet.

She was trembling. It was painful to go on, so keen were the sensations.

"Hal," she cried. "Now, Hal!"

His body leaped suddenly, and Marie heard his muffled gasp as the long-delayed instant of joy reached him. In the same moment, Marie scaled the last peak, and this time all tension dissolved, and the fulfillment was complete, and she sank back limply against the carpet.

Contented.

Delighted.

Exhausted.

They rested. Marie did a lot of thinking while they rested.

He said, "You made your mind about Rio up yet?"

"I'm still considering it," she told him. "But I'll tell you pretty soon."

She balanced all the choices one last time. Then she made her decision. It was the decision that she had known all along that she would make.

She said, "I've got to put through a telephone call now, Hal."

CHAPTER FOURTEEN

Lee Floyd sat in his comfortable and expensive orchestra seat, letting the singing and the dancing slide past his unseeing eyes like so many soap bubbles. He couldn't get interested in the musical at all. But he hadn't really come here expecting to watch the show.

The first act ended about five minutes to ten. There was going to be a fifteen-minute intermission. Floyd left his seat along with everybody else, but instead of moving to the lobby he went around to the side door, one Marie had left by, and stepped out into the street. It was a cool, clear evening. No one had seen him leave the theater. Good, he thought. Good.

"Taxi!" he called.

A cab pulled up. Floyd got in and said, "The Latin Quarter."

The cabbie gave him an odd look. After all, the Latin Quarter was only six or seven blocks from the theater. But Floyd didn't feel like walking, and he had money to burn anyway. The cab moved off.

It was quarter after ten when Floyd entered the night club. The place hadn't really started to fill up, yet. The big crowds would be coming over later, after the theater—the way Floyd had told various people he was doing. Actually, though, he'd be operating on a slightly different time schedule. No one at the Latin Quarter would remember that he had arrived at 10:15 and left before eleven.

He took a table and watched the show for a while. The long-legged showgirls prancing around in skimpy costumes didn't interest him at all. Not when he had Marie to dream about. Had Marie once worked in a place like this? There were some good-looking girls on the stage, Floyd thought, but not one of them could compare with Marie. They were mechanically pretty, as though they had been stamped out by some kind of cookie-cutter. But they didn't have the life or sparkle that Marie had.

Or the figures, for that matter.

He ordered a drink, and cracked a joke or two with the waiter. That registered his presence here. It was important, because this was the key time of his alibi. If anybody called him on his whereabouts this night, he was going to say that he had been at the Latin Quarter till midnight, and if it didn't stand up he'd be in trouble.

He left the drink untouched, of course. He had ordered gin on the rocks, with a water chaser, and he simply drank the water and poured the gin into his water glass. Nobody would be the wiser.

After a little while he got up. He talked to two of the nightclub employees, making sure they'd remember him if they were asked. Then he headed for the john, only instead of using it he slipped out a side exit.

It was 10:45.

"Taxi!" he called.

Another cab came gliding up. "Take me to Pennsylvania Station," Floyd said.

He was there in ten minutes. He slipped into the station quietly, went downstairs to the Long Island Rail Road terminal, and without much fuss got himself aboard the train heading for Hewlett. It was fairly crowded, he saw with relief, so he wouldn't be conspicuous. Plenty of Long Islanders on their way home after Saturday night dinner in the city. He picked up a newspaper and opened it wide, holding it in front of his face.

The train pulled out of the station. Floyd was on his way east to Hewlett, to keep his appointment with

Howard and Ethel Gorman.

He was thinking of Marie.

The trip was a dull one. The train chugged along through one suburban town after another, and at ten of twelve it arrived at the Hewlett station. About a dozen people got off. Floyd walked quietly to the end of the station. At their first meeting, Howard Gorman had briefed him thoroughly on the way to go after he left the depot. It was a fairly short walk from the station to the Gorman home.

Floyd walked briskly down the leafy lanes of the quiet streets. By midnight on the nose he was standing before the shadowy bulk of Howard Gorman's two-story home. It was a big, handsome brick-and-timber place, with the reek of money about it. Two towering trees that looked like they must be hundreds of years old framed the entrance. Quite a place, Floyd thought. The man who lived here must have a load of dough socked away. It was pleasant to contemplate.

He checked his watch. Right on the button. Pretty good timing, Floyd thought. But, then, precision had always been his trademark.

The light was on in the second-floor bedroom, as they had planned. And Gorman was supposed to have arranged it so that the casement window would be open, giving him easy access.

Good old Howard, Floyd thought. *He was very considerate about cooperating in all this.*

He looked up and down the street. Nobody in sight, in any direction.

Floyd began to climb.

It was hand over hand in the darkness, up the rough brick. The old Human Fly routine, but Floyd had practiced it many times. All it took was a good strong set of fingers and lots of guts.

He reached a little balcony and paused there a moment, catching his breath and letting his fingers uncramp. Then he slid his gun out of its holster and pole-vaulted his way into the bedroom, gun first.

A startled-looking woman gaped at him.

"Oh! Who are you?"

Mrs. Ethel Gorman, Floyd thought, looked just about as he had expected her to look. She was graying, portly, flabby around the chin. She seemed to have just come home from a party, because she was expensively dressed, with a glittering array of diamonds twinkling here and there on her clothing.

"Hand over your jewels and you won't get hurt," Floyd said, playing his part to the hilt. "Keep quiet. No noise at all."

He reached a gloved hand for her necklace.

She behaved as expected. Pushing his hand away, she screamed, "Howard! Help, there's a burglar in my bedroom! Howard!"

Floyd shot her.

It was an expertly placed shot, one which he had planned all day and which he executed with slick perfection. He angled the shot up through her body to make it look like a wild slug that had accidentally ripped through her heart—the shot of a panicky, confused burglar.

The shot knocked her down, and she went over like a tenpin and didn't budge. Killed instantly, Floyd figured. Pretty good shooting, for an "accident." Floyd ripped away the necklace, taking care to break the setting and scatter the jewels all over the floor. This was going to look like a thoroughly bungled robbery, by the time it was over. But the cops would certainly send out an alarm for all known second-story men—taking the heat off everybody else.

The bedroom door opened.

Howard Gorman entered. He was gray-faced and sick-looking. He shivered a little as he glanced down at the body on the floor.

"Is she—dead?" he asked. He seemed to have difficulty forcing words up through his constricted throat. He looked so shaken up that Floyd wondered if he'd have a heart attack and drop dead, saving him the trouble of firing another shot.

Floyd nodded. "She's extremely dead. Congratulations, Gorman. You're now a widower, and I've earned my five thousand."

"And I'm free to have Marie," Gorman exulted. His sickly expression faded a little, triumph appearing. "Okay. I'll give you some time to get out of here, and then I'll phone the police. They'll think it was a burglar."

Floyd shook his head. "I'm afraid it isn't going to work out that way, Howard."

"I don't understand you."

Floyd lifted the gun a second time. "I'll spell it out for you," he said softly. "I met Marie. She's quite a girl. I want her too."

"No!"

"Yes," Floyd said. "And I'm afraid I'm the one who gets her."

He fired and Howard Gorman toppled, his face permanently frozen in astonishment. He twitched once, and then he lay still, beside his wife.

There, Floyd thought. Now Marie's mine.

He seemed to feel her soft warmth against him already. The job here was done. Now to get back to the city, wait until it was safe to clear out

The phone rang.

Floyd's kill-hardened nerves kept him from jumping in alarm at the sudden clangor. He stared at the phone, wondering what to do. It continued to ring and ring.

Suddenly he realized that it could only be Marie calling him, to find out how it had gone. Who else would call at this hour? She knew what time the murders were scheduled for! She had no business calling, though. He wasn't going to answer it. He didn't want to talk to her until Monday or Tuesday.

But the phone went on ringing. Maybe it was important, he thought. Something she felt he had to know right away. That detective tipping someone off, maybe?

He snatched up the receiver. "Yes?" he said in a muffled, gruff voice.

"Lee?"

"Yes," he said. "Hello, Marie."

"How did it go?"

"It's all clear now. It's all over."

To his surprise a harsh cackling laugh came over the telephone. "Are they both dead?" Marie asked, breaking into more laughter.

She's hysterical from joy, he thought.

"Yes," he said. "But why did you call?"

"To find out if it was over."

"It is."

"That's great," she said. "Because now Hal and I can take off for South America."

"Hal?" he said, bewildered.

"Thanks, Floyd. Thanks for everything. Including the loving. You were good. Real good, Lee. But you handle a woman the way you'd handle a gun. So long, sucker. And thanks again."

For a crazy second Floyd couldn't understand what she was telling him. Then it sank in. He thought of the high tilted breasts and the soft red hair and the long curvy body, and half a sob escaped him in his fury as he slammed the phone down.

I'll kill 'em both, he thought!

There were plenty of bullets left in the .38. And all he needed was two. He had been insane in the first place to fool around with a woman. His job was to kill, and Marie had tricked him into doing the killing for her, and for that Hal of hers, whoever he was.

He vaulted over the corpses in the bedroom and out onto the little balcony, wondering where he was going to find Marie now. He'd track her down, no matter where she went.

Then he heard the sirens.

They came wailing down the quiet suburban street, and there were dark police cars behind them. Naturally.

Naturally.

Marie had suckered him out completely and utterly, and had finished the job off with one final twist.

Floyd leaped to the ground when he was still ten feet above it, and his foot jammed painfully into the earth. A bolt of fire shot up through his ankle to his knee. He started to run, desperately, across the lawn. Dim shapes were moving across the street. People were shouting things at him. Floyd didn't hear them.

He didn't hear anything, except the mocking laughter of a red-haired temptress who had sold him out.

He thought of this mysterious Hal. Hal was riding high right now, but he'd get his someday. Marie would sell him out, too, when the price was right, the way she had sold out Howard Gorman, the way she had sold out Floyd himself. You just couldn't believe Marie would betray you, until the moment she did.

Poor Hal, he thought. He laughed.

Then the spotlights flashed out, blinding him.

Floyd yanked out his gun and shot three times, wildly, in the general direction of the blazing lights. The cops returned his fire in a blistering volley.

Poor Hal, Floyd thought again.

Poor Gorman.

And poor me.

He laughed again, wildly. He was still laughing when the hot slugs came ripping into him, tearing his life away.

THE END

Robert Silverberg, born January 15, 1935 in New York City, has forged a career as one of science fiction's most respected writers and editors. Author of such seminal works as *Hawksbill Station, Dying Inside, A Time of Changes* and *Downward to the Earth*, as well as  the Majipoor Chronicles, he has also produced innumerable non-fiction works, historical novels and hundreds of erotic books for such publishers as Nightstand, Greenleaf and Midwood Books in the 1950's and early 60's. Writing under a variety of names—including Don Elliott, Loren Beauchamp, David Challon and Mark Ryan—he is one of the most prolific and creative authors of the 20th century. Silverberg lives and continues to write in Oakland, California.

Black Gat Books

Black Gat Books is a new line of mass market paperbacks introduced in 2015 by Stark House Press. New titles appear every other month, featuring the best in crime fiction reprints. Each book is size to 4.25" x 7", just like they used to be, and priced at $9.99 (1–31) and $10.99 (32–). Collect them all.

1 Haven for the Damned
   by Harry Whittington
   978-1-933586-75-5
2 Eddie's World
   by Charlie Stella
   978-1-933586-76-2
3 Stranger at Home
   by Leigh Brackett
   writing as
   George Sanders
   978-1-933586-78-6
4 The Persian Cat
   by John Flagg
   978-1933586-90-8
5 Only the Wicked
   by Gary Phillips
   978-1-933586-93-9
6 Felony Tank
   by Malcolm Braly
   978-1-933586-91-5
7 The Girl on the Bestseller
   List
   by Vin Packer
   978-1-933586-98-4
8 She Got What She Wanted
   by Orrie Hitt
   978-1-944520-04-5
9 The Woman on the Roof
   by Helen Nielsen
   978-1-944520-13-7
10 Angel's Flight
   by Lou Cameron
   978-1-944520-18-2
11 The Affair of Lady
   Westcott's Lost Ruby /
   The Case of the Unseen
   Assassin by Gary Lovisi
   978-1-944520-22-9

12 The Last Notch
   by Arnold Hano
   978-1-944520-31-1
13 Never Say No to a Killer
   by Clifton Adams
   978-1-944520-36-6
14 The Men from the Boys
   by Ed Lacy
   978-1-944520-46-5
15 Frenzy of Evil
   by Henry Kane
   978-1-944520-53-3
16 You'll Get Yours
   by William Ard
   978-1-944520-54-0
17 End of the Line
   by Dolores &
   Bert Hitchens
   978-1-9445205-7
18 Frantic
   by Noël Calef
   978-1-944520-66-3
19 The Hoods Take Over
   by Ovid Demaris
   978-1-944520-73-1
20 Madball
   by Fredric Brown
   978-1-944520-74-8
21 Stool Pigeon
   by Louis Malley
   978-1-944520-81-6
22 The Living End
   by Frank Kane
   978-1-944520-81-6
23 My Old Man's Badge
   by Ferguson Findley
   978-1-9445208-78-3

24 Tears Are For Angels
   by Paul Connelly
   978-1-944520-92-2
25 Two Names for Death
   by E. P. Fenwick
   978-195147301-3
26 Dead Wrong
   by Lorenz Heller
   978-1951473-03-7
27 Little Sister
   by Robert Martin
   978-1951473-07-5
28 Satan Takes the Helm
   By Calvin Clements
   978-1-951473-14-3
29 Cut Me In
   by Jack Karney
   978-1-951473-18-1
30 Hoodlums
   by George Benet
   978-1-951473-23-5
31 So Young, So Wicked
   by Jonathan Craig
   978-1-951473-30-3
32 Tears of Jessie Hewett
   by Edna Sherry
   978-1-951473-36-5
33 Repeat Performance
   by William O'Farrell
   978-1-951473-42-6
34 the Girl With No Place to
   Hide
   by Marvin Albert
   978-1-951473-49-5
35 Gang Rumble
   By Edward Aarons
   978-1-951473-53-2

Stark House Press

1315 H Street, Eureka, CA 95501 707-498-3135
griffinskye3@sbcglobal.net www.starkhousepress.com
Available from your local bookstore or direct from the publisher.